DELORES FOSSEN

SAVIOR IN THE SADDLE

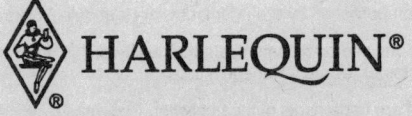
HARLEQUIN®

TORONTO • NEW YORK • LONDON
AMSTERDAM • PARIS • SYDNEY • HAMBURG
STOCKHOLM • ATHENS • TOKYO • MILAN • MADRID
PRAGUE • WARSAW • BUDAPEST • AUCKLAND

To my daughter, Beth

Recycling programs
for this product may
not exist in your area.

ISBN-13: 978-0-373-69509-6

SAVIOR IN THE SADDLE

ABOUT THE AUTHOR

Imagine a family tree that includes Texas cowboys, Choctaw and Cherokee Indians, a Louisiana pirate and a Scottish rebel who battled side by side with William Wallace. With ancestors like that, it's easy to understand why Texas author and former air force captain Delores Fossen feels as if she were genetically predisposed to writing romances. Along the way to fulfilling her DNA destiny, Delores married an air force top gun who just happens to be of Viking descent. With all those romantic bases covered, she doesn't have to look too far for inspiration.

Books by Delores Fossen

HARLEQUIN INTRIGUE

CAST OF CHARACTERS

Sheriff Brandon Ruiz—This small-town Texas sheriff is stunned to learn that he's about to become a father.

Willa Marks—A Texas maternity hostage who's now on the run. Willa's short-term-memory loss makes it impossible for her to know whom to trust, including the father of her child.

Sergeant Cash Newsome—A San Antonio cop and Brandon's longtime friend, but it's possible Cash has his own agenda when it comes to finding out what really happened to the maternity hostages on that fateful day.

Martin Shore—The cold-blooded assassin who's after Willa, but no one knows who hired him.

Lieutenant Bo Duggan—Lead investigator for the maternity hostage situation. Bo's wife died during the hostage situation, and he believes Willa's broken memories hold the secrets to finding all the people responsible for his wife's death.

Doctor Lenora Farris—A psychiatrist who works closely with the police.

Dean Quinlan—The CSI who resigned shortly after the hostage incident. Was it because he had something to hide?

Wes Dunbar—Nightclub owner who might have murdered his rival and then tried to cover it up by orchestrating the maternity hostage situation.

"Just let me go," she begged Brandon. "If this is really your child as you say, then please help me get away."

"It is my child. And I can't let you leave."

"Swear it," she said, sounding as desperate as she felt. "Swear on my life that the baby is yours."

Brandon put his fingers beneath her chin and lifted it to make direct eye contact. "I swear on your life. On mine. On our baby's life. The child you're carrying is mine."

He sounded so sincere. Looked it, too. Still, there was something, something she couldn't quite put her finger on.

"If you're lying to me—"

But Willa didn't get a chance to finish that threat. There was no warning. No time to get down.

A bullet slammed through the bathroom window.

Chapter One

They had found her.

Willa Marks saw the proof of that when the man stepped from the black four-door Ford that had just pulled into her driveway.

He had a badge clipped to his belt.

She pressed her fingers to her mouth to silence the gasp that nearly escaped from her throat and she eased down the blinds that she'd lifted a fraction so she could peek out.

Oh, God.

This couldn't be happening.

Willa hurried away from the window and to the wall next to the door. Her shoulder brushed against the trio of yellow sticky notes that she'd left there, and one of them fluttered to the floor.

Don't Trust the Cops, the note said.

She no longer needed the reminder. At least, Willa didn't think she did. But she'd left it there just in case. It was too important for her to forget something like that again.

"It'll be okay," she whispered to her unborn child, hoping she wasn't lying to the baby and herself.

She slid her hand over her pregnant belly, but she knew her hand wouldn't be much protection if this turned out to be the start of another round in the nightmare that just would not end.

The doorbell rang, the sound knifing through the room, and this time she wasn't able to muffle her gasp. Of course, she'd known they would ring the bell. And they wouldn't stop until she let them inside.

They had found her.

Well, by God, they weren't taking her back into their so-called protective custody. Look where that had gotten her the last two times.

She and her baby had nearly been killed.

There were ten notes around the house to remind her of that, and just in case that wasn't enough, the warning scrolled across the screen saver of her laptop: Don't Trust the Cops.

The doorbell rang again, and it was followed by a heavy knock. "Ms. Marks, I'm Lieutenant Bo Duggan from San Antonio P.D. I know you're in there."

Maybe he had seen her car in the garage. Or perhaps he'd even spotted her when she'd made a quick trip just a half hour earlier to the grocery store.

But how exactly had they found her?

She'd been so careful—using an alias, paying only with cash, leaving no paper trail. She hadn't wanted to dye her hair because of the chemicals, but she hadn't cut it in months and, with it pulled back from her face, she didn't resemble the photos that had been snapped of her four months earlier and splattered all over the news.

Apparently all those safety measures hadn't been enough.

"Lieutenant Bo Duggan," she repeated under her breath, and Willa hurried to grab her PDA from her desk next to the sofa.

There was another knock, and another, but Willa ignored them and scrolled through the pictures and names she'd assembled in case her memory failed her again. She found him. Bo Duggan's photo was there, and she'd added a caption: I Think I Can Trust Him.

It was the word *think* that kicked up her heartbeat an extra notch. But then, in the past four months, there was no one that she trusted completely.

Not even herself.

"We need to talk to you," Lieutenant Duggan said from the other side of the door. "We know you're scared, but there are things we have to ask you—important things."

Willa carried the PDA back to the window and peeked out again. The lieutenant's face matched the picture she had, but he wasn't alone.

There was another man with him.

The second man was tall and lanky. He wore jeans and a crisp, white shirt topped with a buckskin jacket, and he held a saddle-brown Stetson in his left hand. His dress was casual, unlike the lieutenant who had on a dark blue suit.

It was the second man that Willa focused on. Did she know him?

His face wasn't familiar.

He had thick black hair that was slightly long and rumpled, no doubt from the cold December wind that was assaulting them. With that Stetson, jeans and jacket, he looked like a cowboy from the *Texas Monthly* magazine she had on her coffee table.

His skin was deeply tanned, but she shook her head, rethinking that. The skin tone was probably natural. Those high cheekbones and features were Native American.

She frantically scrolled through the pictures again, but she didn't expect to find him. With those unique looks, Willa thought he might be someone she would remember without the prompts, pictures and captions.

"Ms. Marks," the lieutenant tried again. "Please, open the door."

The knocks got harder, and each blow against the thick wood sent her pulse racing out of control. She couldn't call the local cops. There were plenty of notes telling her not to trust them. So maybe she could wait out these two. Eventually Lieutenant Duggan and his Native American partner would get tired of knocking and leave.

She hoped.

Then she could gather her things and go on the run again.

The baby inside her kicked hard, as if protesting that. "Well, I'm not too happy about it, either," Willa mumbled.

She'd lived here at this suburban Austin rental house for two months now, and that was a month longer than the extended-stay hotel where she'd stayed in Houston.

Two months hadn't been long enough for her to settle in or to stop being afraid, but she had started to believe she might be able to remain here until after the baby was born. Or at least until Christmas, which was only three days away.

So much for her short-term dreams.

They were as fleeting as her short-term memory had been just weeks ago.

"Willa?" someone called out.

Not the lieutenant. Another look out the blinds, and she realized it was the other man who'd spoken. The man whose picture wasn't in her PDA. But he had said her name as if he knew her.

No, it was more than that.

He said her name as if he knew her *intimately*.

"Willa, it's me, Brandon. Look, I know you're probably still mad at me—I don't blame you. But I've been searching for you all this time so I could tell you how sorry I am about the argument we had."

"Brandon?" She repeated it several times, but it jogged no memory.

Who was he? What did he want? And what argument had they had? Better yet, just how badly did she need to know the answers to those questions?

Willa made sure all four locks on the front door were engaged, though she already knew they were. That was routine these days. The lights were green on the security panel box, meaning it was armed and ready to sound if tripped. Also routine. As were the window locks, gun and the multiple cans of pepper spray she had stashed around the house.

The lieutenant and his partner couldn't get in. Well,

not unless they broke down the door or smashed a window, but that could happen if she spoke to them or not.

"Do I know you?" she called out. And Willa prayed that merely asking the question wouldn't turn out to be a deadly mistake.

She watched through the blinds, and she saw the men whispering to each other. Both of them also fired glances all around the yard and street. Not ordinary glances, either. The kind that cops made when they were worried they might be ambushed.

Of course, it was also the kind of glances that criminals made to make sure they weren't being watched.

"You know me," the man, Brandon, assured her. He said it with complete confidence, but there was also a tinge of frustration in his voice. "Willa, open the door. I want to see you."

Willa didn't budge. "How do you know me?"

He hesitated. It wasn't just a pause. But definitely a hesitation. She'd lost so much after everything she'd been through, but she'd gained something, too. Willa had gotten very good at reading people.

Brandon was on edge.

"They told me you had memory loss from a fall you took at the hospital, and that you were in a coma for a while," Brandon finally said. "You still don't remember me after all this time?"

No, but she didn't intend to tell him that.

Truth was, she had no memories—*none*—before the nightmare that had happened four months earlier when she and about three dozen other pregnant women and medical staff had been held hostage at gunpoint for hours on the fourth floor at the San Antonio Maternity Hospital. Questioned. Verbally abused. And worse.

People had died that day, and those who had survived did not come out unscathed.

She was proof of that.

The gunmen had even forced her to help them retrieve some computer files in the lab. Or so she'd been told because part of the hostage standoff had been captured on a hospital surveillance camera.

Willa had no recollection of that, either.

No memories before that fall she'd supposedly taken when one of the gunmen had pushed her down during her attempted escape. No memories before or immediately following the coma she'd supposedly been in when her brain had swollen from a deep concussion.

And what she had remembered since was spotty in too many areas.

The head injury had given her both amnesia and short-term memory loss. That was the last diagnosis she'd received anyway. She hadn't seen a neurologist in nearly a month.

She had made some progress with the short-term memory issues but none with the amnesia itself. She could have indeed met this Brandon, but she knew so few details of her life that anything was possible.

For all practical purposes, Willa's life had begun two months ago when her short-term memory had started to stabilize.

She knew the basics. She was Willa Diane Marks, a computer software designer from San Antonio. Both parents were dead. No living relatives. She wasn't rich, but she'd had more than enough money to decide at the age of thirty-three that she wanted to reduce her hours at the business she'd started and have a child. Since she hadn't been involved in a relationship at the time, she'd used artificial insemination, which had been done at the very hospital where, three months later, she'd been held hostage.

Willa could thank a nurse at the San Antonio Maternity Hospital for filling her in on those few details. And just so she would remember them, Willa had put them in notes in a computer file. Notes she read daily in case she forgot. Heck, there was even a note to remind herself to read the file.

"Well?" Lieutenant Duggan prompted. "Are you going to let us in? Because I have a warrant and I can break down the door if necessary. I don't want to do that, and I don't think you do either. Am I right?"

She dodged the questions. "Brandon, how do you know me?" Willa countered.

More hesitation. More whispered conversation between the men. Finally, Brandon angled his eyes to the window. Right where she was. As if he'd known all along that she was there.

Brandon's gaze met hers. "Willa, I'm your ex-boyfriend."

Whatever she had expected him to say, that wasn't it.

Her heart went to her knees.

The baby stopped kicking and went still. So did Willa. Her breath lodged somewhere between her lungs and her throat, and she forced herself to exhale so she wouldn't get light-headed. She had enough things against her already without adding that.

"My ex-boyfriend?" she challenged. She had been involved with this man, but there was no photo of him in her PDA? No yellow sticky note with his name on her wall? And he darn sure wasn't in her memory. "Prove it."

"Open the door, and I will." It wasn't exactly a promise, but it was close.

Close enough for Willa to put her PDA aside and grab the .38 handgun she kept on top of the foyer table. Before she could change her mind, she undid the locks, paused the security system and opened the front door. There was still a locked screen door between the men and her, but even through the gray mesh, she could see their faces clearly.

Brandon's eyes were a dark earthy brown.

And much to Willa's surprise, she reacted to him. Or rather her body did. There was deep pull within her.

Attraction, she realized.

She was physically attracted to him. Strange, because it was a new sensation for her. She was certain at one time or another she had been attracted to a man, but she didn't remember this feeling.

"What proof do you have?" Willa immediately asked.

Those rich brown eyes combed over her face, but she couldn't tell what was going through his mind. His gaze dropped to her stomach. Since she was seven months pregnant and huge, it would have been hard not to miss her baby bulge. Then, his attention landed on the .38 Smith & Wesson she had gripped in her hand at her side.

"There's no need for that," Brandon said, his voice

mostly calm. There was still that edge to it. "Neither of us will hurt you."

"Forgive me if I don't believe you," she fired back.

"You have reason not to trust us," Lieutenant Duggan volunteered. "We didn't do a good job of protecting you while you were in the hospital recovering from your head injury."

She nearly laughed. "No. You didn't. A gunman got into my room just two days after the hostages were rescued, and he tried to shoot and kill me."

Willa didn't exactly have memories of that incident, either. Thank God. The memory loss was good for some things, and she didn't need that particular nightmare in her head. But she'd read the reports, over and over, and every time she would forget, she would reread them. She needed to remember that the cops hadn't protected her then. Or now.

The lieutenant nodded. "That gunman was caught. His name was Danny Monroe, and later that same morning when he tried to kill a police captain and another hostage, he was shot. He died in surgery. You don't have to worry about him now."

"Maybe not him. But that wasn't the only attempt made on my life," Willa reminded the lieutenant. "Someone tried to break into the safe house where you had me staying after I got out of the hospital."

"You remember that?" Duggan asked.

"No," Willa reluctantly admitted. "But I haven't had any short-term memory problems for the last two months. I remember everything that's happened during that time, and I remember all the notes I've read about the incident."

And that was the truth. *Almost.*

"We're not sure who tried to get into the safe house," the lieutenant admitted, "but it's still under investigation."

"Well, the investigation can continue without my help." She looked at Brandon who was staring at her. "You said you have proof that you're my ex-boyfriend?"

He nodded and shifted his head against the wind when another cold gust slammed into them. "Can we come in, and I'll show you?"

"You can show me what you have from out there. And you'd better have more than a going-steady ring or a picture from our high school prom."

Even though there was something that made her want to trust, and *believe,* the man. Willa groaned. Hadn't the last four months taught her anything?

Brandon mumbled something she didn't catch, and he reached into his pocket, prompting her to bring up her gun. Lieutenant Duggan's hand went to the butt of his own weapon that was tucked in a shoulder holster inside his jacket.

Brandon held up his hands in a calm-down gesture. "I'm not going for a gun."

But he had one. Willa saw it then. It was in a cowboy-style waist holster that rested low on his hips.

She also spotted the badge clipped to his holster, and she backed up a step.

"You're a cop?" she accused.

Brandon nodded. "Not SAPD though. I'm the sheriff of a small town, Crockett Creek. It's about a half hour from San Antonio."

He was still a lawman. The very people her notes warned her not to trust.

"You didn't remember that Brandon Ruiz is a sheriff?" Lieutenant Duggan asked.

"No," she snapped. "And I think there's a reason for that. You're trying to trick me. You figured if you could convince me that this man, this stranger, is my ex-boyfriend that I would let you in so you could talk me into doing whatever it is that brought you here."

Duggan and Brandon exchanged glances, and it was Brandon who continued. "It's true. We do have things to tell you. Things that could affect your safety—and the baby's." He paused, his gaze heading back in that direction again.

He swallowed hard. And looked away.

So, he couldn't even look her in the eye. Or the belly. He was lying.

"Get off my porch," Willa demanded. "And stay away from me."

"I can't," Brandon said. "I have the proof you want." He took a piece of paper from his pocket.

Willa already had her hand on the door, ready to slam it shut, but that stopped her. "What is that?"

"It's a medical report." Brandon took his time continuing that explanation. "You had an amniocentesis done after the hostage incident."

She had. There were notes about it on her computer. The doctors had been concerned that her injury might have affected the baby, so she'd had the test done to examine the amniotic fluid to make sure all was well.

"What does that have to do with anything?" Willa asked.

Brandon's mouth tightened a little. "We, uh, were able to compare the baby's DNA we got from the amniocentesis results that were on file at the hospital."

Now it was Willa who held up her hand. "Wait just a darn minute. Why were you comparing DNA? I had artificial insemination, and I used an anonymous donor."

"No," Lieutenant Duggan disagreed.

And that one-word denial was all he said for several heart-stopping moments.

"We had the nurse tell you that," the lieutenant explained, "because you were so upset—you were hysterical. The doctors couldn't sedate you because you were in the first trimester of your pregnancy, and they thought you might lose the baby if we couldn't calm you down."

"So, they lied," Brandon added.

Willa moved her hand to her heart to try to steady it. "Lied about what exactly?"

Brandon's gaze came to hers. "There was no artificial insemination, Willa. And that baby you're carrying is *mine*."

Chapter Two

Brandon waited for Willa Marks to grasp what he'd just told her.

It didn't take long. Within seconds, her eyes widened. She went pale, and she inched back farther away from the screen door, no doubt to put some distance between her and them.

She stood there, looking scared, lost and vulnerable in her maternity jeans and dove-gray sweater that seemed to swallow her. She was petite, barely five-three. Hardly big enough to be fighting off bad guys, but she'd had to do too much of that in the past four months.

From the corner of his eye, Brandon saw the lieutenant make another sweeping glance around the yard and street. Brandon did the same. Because it might not be safe for Willa or for them to be standing out here in the open like this.

"You're my baby's father?" Willa questioned. Despite her obvious surprise, there was still a Texas-size dose of suspicion in her expression and her tone.

Her memory might not be in full working gear, but her instincts sure were.

She had a reason to be suspicious.

But Brandon didn't want her suspicions to get her and the baby killed.

"We need to come in," Brandon insisted, and he tried not to make it sound like a question.

He immediately saw the debate in her wide blue eyes. She volleyed glances between Bo Duggan and him before she mumbled something under her breath. She went to the screen door, unlocked it and then stepped back.

She held on to the gun, and Brandon hoped like the devil that he didn't have to wrestle it away from her.

Brandon walked in first, and Bo was right behind him. Bo closed the door, and Brandon immediately felt the warmth from the central heating. But not from their guest.

Willa was glaring at them.

He glanced around. Old habits. He'd been a peace officer for eight years. That was eight years too long to let down his guard. Willa had given no indication that someone was inside holding her hostage, but he needed to make sure that wasn't the case.

The place was small so he didn't have to look too far to take it all in. They were in a living-dining combination area, and there was a modest kitchen through the double doorway near the dining table. In the center of the table was a potted plant that had been decorated with tiny foil Christmas ornaments. No wrapped gifts, and judging from Willa's situation, there probably wouldn't be any.

On the other side of the house, he could see directly into the two bedrooms and the bathroom, with all the doors wide open. Apparently, Willa was trying to minimize the chance that anyone could sneak in through one of the windows without her hearing them.

The place was neat as a pin except for the yellow sticky notes all over the walls and surfaces of the furniture. He spotted one on the hardwood floor and reached down to pick it up.

"Don't trust the cops," he read and passed it to Bo.

Bo glanced at it as well and then looked at her. "I thought you weren't having any more short-term memory loss."

"I'm not. The notes are leftovers from a time when I was having problems. I just haven't gotten around to removing them." Her chin came up, causing her long blondish-brown ponytail to swish. It brushed against her shoulder and settled on the top of her left breast.

Brandon quickly got his attention off that.

Should he go to her, he wondered? Should he try to hug or kiss her? That was something Bo and he hadn't discussed on the ride over, but Brandon wished they had. He knew what he had to say to Willa, what he had to do about her safety situation, but he hadn't given much thought to the personal aspect of this.

Willa held out her hand. "Let me see that DNA report," she insisted.

Brandon walked closer, halving the distance between them and gave it to her.

He watched her read through the report, and with each line her gaze skirted across, her forehead bunched up even more.

"It could be a lie," she concluded, handing it back to him.

"Why would we lie about that?" Bo questioned.

Willa opened her mouth. Then, closed it. She shook her head. "I don't know, but you just admitted you lied four months ago when you had a nurse tell me I was artificially inseminated."

"We did that only because we didn't want you to lose the baby. It worked," Bo insisted. "You settled down, quit asking for Brandon, and you started to heal."

"I asked for him?" She immediately wanted to know.

Brandon let Bo answer. "You did. You wanted to see him because he's your baby's father."

Her accusing gaze came back to Brandon. "Then why weren't you there at the hospital that day, when I was scheduled for my first ultrasound along with some other lab tests?"

"I didn't know about it," Brandon answered.

"SAPD thinks the ultrasound and lab tests were a ploy to get to you the hospital that afternoon because the appointment wasn't on the schedule," Bo explained. "We believe the gunmen called you with the bogus appointments because they'd researched the records of several of the pregnant women, and they knew you were a whiz with computers. They thought you could help them access some files."

"I know all of that," she snapped. "It's in my notes." She pointed to Brandon. "That doesn't explain why you weren't there."

Brandon lifted his shoulder, trying to shrug. "We'd had an argument about a month earlier, and you told me to get out, that it was over between us. I was out of the state at the time, and I didn't know you'd been taken hostage until two days after it ended. By then, you were in protective custody at a secret location."

"He asked for your location," Bo continued. "But there had already been an attempt on your life, and we thought it best if no one knew where you were."

And then there had been another breach of security. Another intruder. That had caused Willa to go on the run, leaving the safe house and not telling anyone where she was. It'd taken SAPD all this time to find her.

Without moving her gaze from Brandon's, she walked closer, her steps slow and deliberate. Until she was very close. So close he could take in her scent. There was some kind of floral fragrance in her hair. Roses, maybe.

She reached out and caught onto his arm. Brandon wasn't sure what she had in mind, but he didn't think she was about to launch herself against him for a welcome-home kiss.

No. Her suspicions were getting stronger.

She took his hand and placed it on her stomach. On the baby.

Brandon pulled in his breath before he could stop himself, but he did manage to hold his ground and not move away. He also kept eye contact with her, which was probably stupid.

Willa didn't say a word. She just stared at him.

The moments crawled by and because Brandon didn't know what the hell else to do he just stood there.

"Let me guess," Willa said, her words as slow and deliberate as her steps had been. "We argued about the baby. That's why we broke up. Because you weren't ready to be a father."

Brandon settled for a nod.

"What was I to you—your one-night stand?" she asked. No more of that slow and deliberate tone. She was riled now.

"No," he answered truthfully. "Willa, you weren't a one-night stand."

She studied his eyes. Then she studied him. Her gaze eased down the length of his body. Back up. And then she groaned, turned and sank down on the sofa. She put the gun on the coffee table, something that probably pleased Bo as much as it did him.

They'd made it past step one.

But they had a hell of a long way to go.

"I'll give you two some time alone," Bo said, hitching his thumb to the door. "I'll be in the car. But just don't take too long."

And Brandon knew why. This was not going to be a lengthy romantic welcome-home chat. They were in a hurry.

Bo opened the door, and the wind cut through the room again. The notes on the walls stirred, and two of them went flying through the air. One of them landed near Brandon's boots.

"Take prenatal vitamins," he read aloud and handed her the note. He eased down into the chair across from her. "Just how bad is your memory?"

"Just how much didn't you want this baby?" Willa countered.

So, her memory wasn't up for discussion. He wished she'd taken the baby talk off the table as well.

Brandon knew they had to discuss it, eventually. That was all part of the plan, but he hadn't counted on having the emotional reaction of touching Willa. And he sure as hell hadn't counted on this gut need to protect her. He'd planned on doing what SAPD wanted and then walking away.

Especially walking away.

He was good at that.

But he'd been in the room with Willa for less than fifteen minutes, and he was already having doubts about this plan. She deserved the truth.

The *whole* truth about why he was there.

"Tell me who you are," she insisted. "Not just your name. I want to know who you really are."

Brandon nodded and gathered his thoughts. "My full name is Brandon Michael Ruiz. Like you, I was born in San Antonio. I'm thirty-six. Never been married. I spent some time in the army before I came back to Texas and made it my home again."

She motioned for him to continue.

"I've been sheriff of Crockett Creek for eight years."

"And your bloodline?"

"My dad was—is," he corrected, "Comanche. My mother was part Irish, part Italian, part German. Guess that makes me a real American, huh?"

Willa ignored his attempt to lighten up the conversation. "How did we meet?"

Thankfully, he didn't have to pause to collect his thoughts. "At a restaurant on the Riverwalk in San Antonio. The place was crowded, and we shared a table."

She stared at him again. "I think you're probably lying about that. I don't know why." She waved him off before he could try to convince her otherwise. "It doesn't matter. It's obvious you don't want to be here so that means the lieutenant brought you to convince me to do something."

Well, he hadn't expected her to give him that kind of opening.

"But first, you're supposed to regain my trust," she continued. "And SAPD's theory is the reason I'll trust you again is that we have a child in common." She moved closer to the edge of the sofa. "But you and I both know how things really are, don't we, Brandon?"

Yeah, he thought, maybe they did, so Brandon stuck with the truth. "I gave up the idea of being a father not long after I got out of the military. Let's just say I didn't think my gene pool was worth passing along to an innocent baby."

She made a sound to indicate she was thinking about that. And he could see the doubt creep back into her eyes. "That probably has something to do with the *was* versus the *is* when you described your father's bloodline, but I don't believe you want to share that secret with me so I won't push."

Surprised, Brandon angled his head to the side and studied her. "Have you been taking deception-training classes since you've been in hiding?"

The corner of her mouth lifted, but the smile didn't make it to her eyes. "When I couldn't remember anything for more than ten minutes, I started relying on other things. Eye contact. Facial signals. My gut instincts," she added in a mumble.

Brandon tried his hand at it. "The way you said the last part—*my gut instincts*—does that mean you don't like what your gut instincts are telling you about me?"

Her glare returned. "Stand up," she said abruptly.

"Excuse me?"

"Stand up. *Please*." That last word was clearly an afterthought.

Brandon did stand, all the while wondering where this would lead. And Willa stood up as well. She went to him, hesitating just a second, before she reached up and caught on to the back of his neck. She pulled him down and touched her mouth to his.

It was a peck, hardly qualifying as a kiss, but it lit a very bad fire inside him that shouldn't be lit. A fire below the belt.

She pulled back and drew her tongue over her bottom lip. Yet something to stoke that blaze that he had to put out.

"Yes," she said, "I think I remember kissing you." Willa shook her head, stared up at him.

Brandon decided to do something to convince her to reconsider that *I think* part. His hand went to her back, and he hauled her to him.

And he kissed her.

Yeah, it was probably stupid, but he didn't keep it a peck or at some wimp level to be merely a test. No. He wanted this to be a kiss she'd remember. So, he pressed his lips against hers, moving over her mouth. Taking in her taste, along with that incredible scent. He got an even better sample of her when his tongue touched hers.

She jerked away from him and stepped back. Way back. Her breath was gusting now. Brandon realized his was, too. And she propped her hands on her hips and stared at him.

"I'm attracted to you," she said in the same tone as if confessing to premeditated murder.

The woman certainly knew how to keep him on his toes. "I'm attracted to you," he echoed.

Her stare turned to another glare. "I hate that I just told you that because it gives you leverage over me. But don't be fooled." Willa walked to the foyer table and grabbed her PDA. "I will never put anything I feel for you over the safety of my baby. That means I'm not going to let you talk me into doing anything I could regret."

Oh, man. Since they kept going back to that, Brandon figured it was time to move on to step two.

At least step two didn't involve kissing her.

"The baby is my priority, too," he clarified. "Yeah, I know. I said I'd dismissed fatherhood, but now that I know a baby's on the way—"

"It's a girl," Willa interrupted. "I'm having a daughter."

It took everything inside him not to react. He nodded. "A daughter," he repeated.

Brandon eased that information aside and got back to work.

Yes, he still wanted to protect Willa. He was sorry for what she'd been through. But the groundwork had been laid. She'd bought the story, and it was time to move on. However, before he could do that, Willa lifted the PDA and a second later, there was a small burst of light.

She took his picture.

She typed in something. Paused. And added something else. Notes about him no doubt.

Don't Trust Brandon Ruiz maybe.

Well, she would have to learn to trust him. At least temporarily.

"You're going to have to leave this place and come with me," he told her. Willa started to object, but Brandon talked right over her. "You don't have a choice. The baby's safety is at stake, and I won't let you endanger my child."

There. That was the gauntlet.

"*Your* child?" she said, mocking him.

"Oh, no, we're not going back to that part about my ambivalence toward fatherhood. We'll do what's best for this baby. And what's best is for you not to be here."

Willa didn't say a word, not even to demand more information. She was no doubt trying to figure out how she could escape. That attempt would probably come when she tried to excuse herself to go to the bathroom. Or to get something from the kitchen.

But that wasn't going to happen.

"We've received an intelligence report that there's going to be another hostage situation," Brandon stated as clearly as he could.

Her bottom lip started to tremble. "Where?" Her voice was all breath.

"We don't know that. Or when. Or who will be involved. All we have is that it'll take place at an undisclosed hospital and that the person responsible has hired two computer techs to break into some files."

She caught her bottom lip between her teeth to stop

the trembling. From what he'd been told, Willa didn't have any actual memories of the hostage situation she'd endured, but she had read reports. Heck, she'd probably memorized them and knew she didn't want any other person to go through what she had.

"You could put guards at all the hospitals," Willa suggested.

He shook his head. "Too many of them. We can put them on alert, of course, and warn them of the potential danger, but we're not even sure this attack will happen at a hospital in the state. It could happen anywhere."

She waited a moment. Mumbled something. "How can I help?" she finally asked.

Brandon took a deep breath. Even though he still had to be mindful of her attempted escape, step two had been a success. Now, it was time for the grand finale.

Well, part of it anyway.

The last step wouldn't happen until SAPD was sure this new hostage threat had been squelched.

"We think someone masterminded the situation with the maternity hostages," he continued.

"But you caught the two gunmen and the man who hired them. I read about it."

"Yes, his name was Gavin Cunningham, and last week he committed suicide in prison. In his suicide note he indicated he hadn't worked alone, that someone had helped him set up the entire maternity hostage situation."

The breath rushed from her mouth. "Who helped him?"

"We're not sure. That's where we're hoping you can fill us in."

"I get it," she said almost immediately. "You want me to resume my therapy so I can remember if the gunman who held me said anything about the identity of his boss."

"Yeah."

Among other things.

"But I might not remember," she pointed out. "Or maybe the gunman didn't say anything to me at all. I could be putting myself out there for no reason."

"You wouldn't be just putting yourself out there, Willa." Brandon tried to keep his voice level and calm. "I'd be with you. You'd be in my protective custody."

She rolled her eyes. "Let me guess—that wasn't your idea. It was Lieutenant Duggan's."

Brandon evaded that. "Bo Duggan lost his wife during that hostage situation. She died after giving birth to their twins. He's, well, eager to solve this case once and for all."

She stayed quiet a moment. Then, she said, "No."

"No?" Brandon challenged. Well, there went his calm and level voice.

"No," she insisted. "I won't go with you into protective custody. And I won't work directly with Lieutenant Duggan, SAPD or even you."

She pointed to her laptop. Don't Trust the Cops was scrolling across the screen in bold white letters on black background.

She had a reason not to trust cops, or anyone else for that matter. But he had to get her past that because she had no choice. Willa had to trust him.

Even if he didn't deserve that trust.

"I'll restart my therapy on my own," she continued.

"I can't take any memory-activating drugs because they might harm the baby, but maybe hypnosis will work if I try it again. I can do the hypnosis sessions here."

Brandon shook his head. "No, you can't."

That got her back on her feet. "Now, just a darn minute. You might be my baby's biological father and my former boyfriend, but that doesn't give you any say in my life."

He got to his feet as well. "This badge does."

She pulled back her shoulders and looked as if he slapped her. "You're pulling rank on me?"

"I don't have a choice, Willa." He'd practiced this on the drive over, but he didn't think practice would make it sound any better than it had when he'd first said it. "We didn't just get intel about another hostage situation. We learned from a deep-cover agent that an assassin has been hired."

Her shoulders went back even further. "An assassin?"

He nodded and relied on the words he'd rehearsed. "An assassin hired to come after you."

Oh, man. She didn't just pale, every drop of color drained from her face. Willa slipped her PDA into the pocket of her sweater, sank back onto the sofa and buried her face in her hands.

Brandon went in for the kill. He had to tell her the final part of this covert briefing. The detail that would put her back in police custody.

And maybe right back in danger.

"That's how we knew where to find you," Brandon said, hating the sound of his own voice and the words coming out of his mouth.

Chapter Three

Willa was glad she was sitting down.

She didn't speak—she couldn't—and she didn't look at Brandon. Instead, she forced herself to focus on what he'd just told her.

An assassin would come tonight to kill her.

Maybe.

The warning on her screen saver flashed in her head, and it was the reminder she needed to put this in perspective.

"Is it true?" she asked, with her eyes still turned away from Brandon. She wanted to listen for the inflection in his voice.

"It's true, an assassin plans to kill you. We think because his boss doesn't want to risk your memory recovering so you can tell the authorities his identity. But I'm going to protect you," Brandon quickly added. "Because you'll gather your things and come with me. I've already arranged a place for you."

Her emotions were like a whirlwind inside her, but she thought he might be telling the truth about the assassin. There was some kind of danger anyway. Brandon definitely wasn't lying about that.

Willa wasn't naive enough to believe she'd be able to keep out a professional killer. All the security precautions she had already taken wouldn't be enough, and the last thing she wanted was to go gun to gun with an assassin. The three-hour handgun course was her only training with a firearm, and she was betting the man coming after her would know how to kill with one shot.

She nodded, stood and rubbed her hands on the sides of her jeans. "Give me a minute, please. I need some time to gather my thoughts."

And her things.

She had an emergency bag already packed and stashed beneath her bed, and she'd practiced climbing out the window. She could cut through the backyard and walk to the train station, which was only four blocks away. That's one of the reasons she'd chosen this particular house to rent.

Willa headed for her bedroom, but she didn't get far. Brandon was right behind her. She whirled around, not realizing he was so close, and she knocked right into him. The contact was a reminder of that kiss, and the fact that he was going to be a hard man to shake.

"I can't let you escape," he told her.

"Who said I'm trying to escape?" Willa tossed right back.

He gave her a flat look to indicate he knew what she had in mind. Probably did, too. He was a cop, after all.

"Lieutenant Duggan is watching the back of the house, so you wouldn't get far anyway," Brandon added. "Now, get your things so we can leave."

Willa considered arguing with him, but he looked as stubborn as she was. Not a good DNA legacy to pass on to their daughter. A double dose of bullheadedness.

If he was the baby's father, that is.

She wasn't convinced he'd told her the truth about that, either.

"I'll get my things," she agreed. But that was the only thing she was agreeing to do. She wasn't going with them, and that meant she had to distract Brandon in some way so she could escape.

"What did you type about me on your PDA?" he asked, following her into the bedroom. There was barely enough space for one person, and she was quickly learning that Brandon had a way of monopolizing not just the room but all the air in it.

"Nothing," she lied. And she grabbed the packed overnight bag, put it on the bed and tossed in the PDA. The bag already contained a change of clothes, toiletries, meds, cash, a fake ID that had cost her dearly and a flash drive with duplicate files that were on her computer.

She also had a gun in there.

Willa didn't want to use it, but she would if it came down to protecting her baby.

Because she wanted to buy some time for that escape opportunity, Willa went through the dresser drawer and pretended to look for something to add to the bag. Maybe conversation would help, too. Besides, there was one thing she needed to verify, even though she wasn't sure a chat with Brandon would give her that proof.

"Are you really my baby's father?" she asked.

But he didn't answer. He walked across the room

and looked into the drawer to see what she was doing. He likely thought she had a gun and was maybe about to pull it on him. No gun. However, he took the tiny canister of pepper spray from the top of the dresser and cupped it in his hand.

Willa gave him a cynical smile. "You trust me about as much as I trust you. So answer my question. Are you really my baby's father?"

He looked her straight in the eyes.

And nodded.

"The DNA test is real," he said. "The child you're carrying is mine."

Everything inside her went still. Because that didn't sound like a lie.

"We were in love?" she pressed.

"No," he answered just as quickly.

That seemed to be the truth as well. Strange that he wouldn't have said yes and then used that love confession to convince her to cooperate with him.

"All right." For show, she took out several pairs of panties and shoved them into the bag. "So, we weren't in love, and I wasn't your one-night stand. What was I to you?"

"The same thing you are to me now." He didn't wait for her to respond to that puzzling answer. "Finish packing."

She added a bra to the bag and stuffed in a flannel nightgown. Willa lifted the bag and put the strap over her like a messenger's bag even though it was a tight fit over her belly. "I have to get some things from the bathroom. Prenatal vitamins," she added, knowing he wouldn't refuse to let her get those.

The bathroom window was small, but she knew she could squeeze through it. She'd have to hurry and hope that Lieutenant Duggan wasn't keeping watch on that particular side of the house. All she needed was two minutes, and she could be out of there. Away from the assassin, and away from the cops—including, perhaps, her baby's father.

And that gave her an idea.

With Brandon right on her heels, she went into the bathroom and took out a cotton swab from the medicine cabinet. It obviously wasn't sterile, but she thought it would give her a clean enough sample. After all, labs got DNA from toothbrushes and baby bottles. Once she had his DNA extracted, she could have it compared to the baby's amniotic fluid. Willa didn't have the fluid itself, but she had her baby's DNA profile in an online storage file that she could retrieve from any computer.

Of course, a comparison would take days. Maybe longer. Still, she would eventually know one way or another.

Her gut was already telling her the test was unnecessary, that Brandon was indeed her baby's father. But her brain wanted to know why her gut trusted this man when it was clear that he wasn't volunteering the whole truth.

"Open your mouth please." She added the *please* hoping it would get him to cooperate.

He did. Brandon swabbed the inside of his left cheek and handed it back to her. "It'll be a match," he promised.

"We'll see."

He glanced at the swab. "You'll want to put that in a plastic bag." And he pulled a small evidence baggie from his jacket pocket.

Willa eyed him and the bag with suspicion, and instead of using his bag that might be contaminated with his DNA or something else, she headed to the kitchen and got a plastic sandwich bag. She sealed up the swab, put it in the overnight case and snapped her fingers.

"Prenatal vitamins," she said as if remembering them. "I wouldn't want to forget those."

She took slow steps, trying to get the timing of this just right. She needed to get to the bathroom just ahead of Brandon so she could slam the door. Lock it.

And escape.

"I also have to use the bathroom," she lied when she was a few steps away. "As in, actually *use* the bathroom. I don't want an audience for that."

She went inside and pushed the door so it would close.

Brandon caught it.

"I don't want an audience," she restated.

"And I don't want you trying to escape. Don't worry. I'll close my eyes. But this door is staying partly open."

Great. Just great. She hadn't wanted to do this, but she was obviously going to have to give him a hit of the pepper spray. She reached into her bag to retrieve it, but he caught her wrist.

Then he grabbed the bag.

"I'll hold this for you. It can't be good for a pregnant woman to carry around this much weight."

"It's not that heavy." Willa glared at him and kept a firm hold on her bag. "Why don't you just back off?"

"Because I can't. Forget about the personal connection we have because of the baby, forget about how you feel or don't feel about me. Just remember, I'm a lawman, and I'm not going to stand by and let that assassin come after you."

She had to tamp down her anger so she could try to reason with him. "The last two times I trusted a lawman, I was nearly killed. You know that. You've read the reports. I've done a lot better on my own."

"But you've never come up against a hired gun like Martin Shore. He's not someone you can get away from without help."

For some reason having the name attached to the assassin made her heart pound even harder. "Martin Shore," she repeated. "How did he even find me?"

"Apparently Shore's boss has been trying to track you through neurologists all over the state. Nearly a dozen doctors have had their files hacked. Including Dr. Betterman, the OB you saw four weeks ago."

She shook her head. "But I didn't use my real name, and I paid him in cash."

"You did, but in your hacked medical record, Dr. Betterman had written your diagnosis of post-traumatic amnesia and post-concussional neurosis resulting in short-term memory loss. He also listed your age, the date of the onset of the symptoms. And that you were in your third trimester of pregnancy and therefore couldn't receive traditional medications."

Oh, God.

There wouldn't have been many patients who fit into all those categories.

Then, Willa remembered something. "I didn't give the doctor my street address. He said he needed to mail me the results from my latest EEG, so I gave him the address of the rental box at a private mail facility all the way across town."

Brandon nodded. "The clerk there was murdered about four hours ago. We're pretty sure after he was tortured before he gave up your physical address to someone who wanted to find you. Because it was about an hour later when a deep-cover agent intercepted the intel about Shore being hired to kill you."

Willa choked back another *Oh, God,* and the tears that threatened to follow. She wouldn't cry. It would only waste time because she knew what she had to do.

"Just let me go," she begged Brandon. "If this is really your child as you say, then please help me get away."

"It *is* my child. And I can't let you leave."

"Swear it," she said, sounding as desperate as she felt. "Swear on my life that the baby is yours."

Brandon put his fingers beneath her chin and lifted it to make direct eye contact. "I swear on your life. On mine. On our baby's life. The child you're carrying is mine."

He sounded so sincere. Looked it, too. Still, there was something, something she couldn't quite put her finger on.

"If you're lying to me—"

But Willa didn't get a chance to finish that threat. There was no warning. No time to get down.

A bullet slammed through the bathroom window.

Chapter Four

Brandon latched on to Willa and pushed her out of the bathroom.

It wasn't a second too soon because there was another shot ripping through what was left of the glass in the small window. He drew his gun and maneuvered her into the living room and then to the kitchen. He wanted her as far away from those shots as he could manage.

Hell.

He hadn't expected the attack to come this soon. He'd hoped to have Willa tucked safely away before Martin Shore tried to kill her. Brandon obviously hadn't succeeded, and Willa might pay the price for his miscalculation.

Brandon used his phone to call for backup from the Austin P.D. He couldn't risk trying to ring Bo because his temporary partner might be trying to conceal his location from the shooter.

Willa grabbed a knife and a can of pepper spray from the counter and covered her pregnant belly with her hand. Neither her hand nor the items would provide the baby with much protection, so Brandon threw open the fridge and positioned her behind the door. That would give her an extra layer. He considered pulling out the fridge and placing her in the space behind it, but if Shore moved to that side of the house, the bullets might make it through the wall.

"You weren't lying," Willa mumbled.

Not about Shore, he wasn't. But he had told her lies all right. Later, much later, he needed to fill her in on the whole truth.

There was another shot, not through the bathroom. There was the sound of more glass shattering, and it seemed to be coming from Willa's bedroom.

Brandon waited. Listening.

Where the hell was Bo? And better yet, where had the lieutenant been when that first shot had been fired? Brandon hoped Shore hadn't managed to injure Bo or worse.

Another sound, not a bullet this time, sent Brandon's heart to his knees. Because this one had come from inside. From Willa's bedroom. It was the sound of footsteps.

The assassin was in her house.

Brandon glanced at Willa. Her eyes were wide, and her breath was gusting. She'd obviously heard the footsteps, too, and she knew the danger was bearing down on them.

He couldn't wait for word from Bo or for backup to arrive. Once Shore made it to the tiny kitchen, he would see them immediately. They would be sitting ducks, and that meant Brandon had to act fast to keep Willa alive.

"This way," he mouthed.

Brandon kept his gun ready and aimed at the opening

that led from the dining room and into the kitchen. No doubt that was where Shore was headed. He maneuvered Willa behind him so he could shield her with his body, and he started to back them out of the room. It wasn't the best of plans because Shore could double back or even have an accomplice who could come from the other direction, but Brandon had no choice.

He had to get Willa out of there.

Each step seemed to take minutes, but he led them across the kitchen and toward the tiny mudroom and the back door. He wasn't sure what was on the other side of that door, but hopefully it was a yard with some kind of cover. He needed to get Willa behind a tree or something to shelter her from the bullets that would come at them when Shore realized they were no longer inside.

They made it to the opening of the mudroom where they heard a plinking noise as if something metal had been dropped.

Brandon glanced back into the dining room and soon noticed something he didn't want to see: the small, dark green oval object on the floor.

A grenade.

"Run!" Brandon shouted.

Willa reacted fast, thank God. With the knife and pepper spray in her left hand, she pushed her messenger's bag out of the way, disengaged the locks and threw open the door. Brandon had one last look to make sure Shore wasn't about to gun them down from inside the house, and changed places with Willa, so he could be in front of her. Either position was a risk because it was possible the grenade was a decoy to get them to run. If so, they were about to run directly into a professional assassin.

They hurried out onto a small porch and down the steps that led into a yard. No trees, something that made Brandon curse. But there was a small storage shed. He grabbed Willa's arm and made a beeline for it.

There was no sign of Bo. No sign of backup, either, but then it'd only been a couple of minutes since he'd made the call requesting help. Bo had likely called, too.

Well, Bo would have if he wasn't lying dead somewhere.

Shore could have managed to take out Bo before he started the attack on the house.

Brandon hated to force Willa to run, but he had no choice. He prayed this exertion wouldn't hurt the baby. Of course, the stress couldn't be good for the child, either. But Brandon also pushed that aside. Right now, he had to keep Willa alive because it was the only way to save the child.

He positioned Willa to the side of the small wooden shed.

Just as the explosion ripped through the yard.

Brandon had considered that the grenade might be a dummy, but it obviously wasn't.

The debris from the blast came right at them.

Brandon tried to keep watch, to make certain Shore hadn't come into the yard for another attack, but it was hard to see anything. The left side of the house was literally a fireball, and bits of wood, the roof and even wads of fire were raining down on them.

His instincts and training were to protect his fellow

peace officer, but Brandon couldn't risk taking Willa closer to the house. There could be a secondary explosion, and he needed to put some distance between the burning building and her.

Thankfully, she still had the bag draped across her body, and she used it to shelter her face from the dangerous falling debris.

"Is there a gate on the back fence?" he asked her.

She nodded, tried to speak, but no sound came out. Willa was obviously terrified, and there was nothing he could do to assure her that he could protect her. Shore could have orchestrated this entire attack just to get them out in the open.

And the *open* was where they'd have to go to get to the gate.

Brandon checked the strips of grass and shrubs that made up the side yards. No one was there that he could see. No one was on the porch, either, and it was too much to hope that Shore had blown up with that grenade. No. The man was out there, somewhere, waiting.

"Let's go," he told Willa.

As he'd done in the kitchen, Brandon kept in front of her and backed her toward the gate. The debris continued to fall, and he could hear neighbors shouting for help. What he couldn't hear was Bo or the sound of sirens from backup. Until he had help, he had to do everything within his power to get Willa away from there.

Thick black smoke billowed out from the house, fanning out across the yard, and making it impossible for Brandon to see all the places where Shore could be hiding. He kept his gun aimed. Ready.

He saw the movement just at the edge of the smoke. It was a man. And it wasn't Bo. Brandon recognized him from intelligence photos.

It was Martin Shore.

The killer was there, coming for them.

Behind him, Willa fumbled with the gate to open it. She'd obviously put some kind of lock on it, and that lock was now a trap.

Brandon protected Willa as best he could, but he couldn't help with the locks. He kept his eyes and gun trained on Shore and was ready to push Willa to the ground if necessary. That wouldn't take her out of the line of fire, but it might shield her long enough until backup arrived. By now, all the neighbors and anyone for blocks around had probably called for help or come out of their residences to see what was going on.

And what was going on was that Shore was about to try to kill them again.

The man kept walking but lifted his gun, aiming it at them.

Willa cursed, but she must have finally gotten the locks to cooperate because she shoved open the gate. In the same motion Brandon pushed her through to the other side.

A bullet slammed into the fence.

The shot came so close to Brandon's head that he swore he could feel it.

He jumped out of the way, staying low and lunged out of the yard to join Willa on the other side. They made it to a sidewalk that was rimmed with a street and then another row of pristine suburban houses. They could try to duck into one of them, but that wouldn't stop Shore. He'd just fire into the place and possibly kill some innocent bystanders.

"We have to run," Brandon told her. He didn't wait for her to do that. He put his left hand on her shoulder to get her moving, away from the fence and away from her burning house.

Running might not even be possible for someone in the last trimester of pregnancy, but he had to get her to cover so he could try to make a stand against Shore.

Brandon headed up the sidewalk toward the cul de sac where a car was parked. That was their best bet.

Until he saw the kids.

There were three of them, all on skates, and probably no more than ten or eleven years old. If he went in that direction, so would Shore's bullets.

"Get down!" Brandon shouted to the boys. Hopefully they and anyone else in the area would do as he'd ordered.

"This way," Willa insisted, turning and leading him in the opposite direction.

She obviously realized the danger to the children, but she also had to know the danger of going past her house again. Shore had probably made it across the yard by now, and if he wasn't already at the gate, he soon would be.

Brandon adjusted his gun, and aimed, and they hurried past Willa's section of the fence. The smoke was thicker now, and the wind was carrying it right in their direction. Willa coughed, but she didn't stop.

He didn't want to think of the risk this might be

causing the baby. Brandon only wanted to get her out of there. Their best option was the intersection just ahead. Cars were trickling past, but if he could get Willa to that point, he could position her on the side of the last stretch of fence and perhaps get her out of Shore's line of sight.

Brandon heard the creak of the wooden gate and glanced over his shoulder just as it opened.

Shore came out, and he had his gun ready.

The assassin glanced around and spotted them. Brandon wanted to shoot him then and there, but he couldn't risk a stray shot hitting the children.

Shore obviously didn't feel the same. He reaimed, pointing the gun directly at Willa.

Brandon grabbed on to her waist and shoved her into the side of the fence.

A bullet flew past them.

God knew where it landed, and Brandon prayed it hadn't gone into one of the houses or a car.

"We can't stop," he told Willa, though he could hear her breathing hard.

They headed up the street toward a parked car, but then Brandon spotted the city bus. It was only about two blocks away and was lumbering in their direction. If he could get Willa on that bus before Shore saw them, they might be able to escape before the man could figure out where to aim more of those deadly shots.

Brandon kept Willa positioned behind him, and he hurried toward the bus. He also pushed back his jacket to reveal his badge.

"Get back inside!" he shouted to an elderly woman who opened her door.

Still hurrying toward the bus, Brandon flagged down the driver and hoped like the devil the man would stop. He didn't take his attention off the intersection where he knew Shore would soon appear.

The assassin wouldn't just give up.

The bus inched closer, and with Willa in tow, Brandon raced toward the vehicle. The seconds clicked off in Brandon's head. He wanted to make sure these seconds weren't their last ones.

The driver slowed even more as he approached them. Probably because he was concerned about the gun Brandon was holding.

"Open up!" Brandon told the middle-aged Hispanic driver. And he flashed his badge again.

The door swung open.

Just as Brandon caught a glimpse of Shore.

The assassin was at the intersection, barely a block away. Willa was still in Shore's kill zone.

Brandon pushed her onto the bus and was relieved that they were the sole passengers.

"I'm Sheriff Ruiz," he said identifying himself. "Drive!" Brandon ordered the man behind the wheel.

He dragged Willa to the bus's floor, praying that Shore hadn't seen him.

But he obviously had.

Because a bullet came crashing through the bus window.

Chapter Five

Willa covered her head with the bag when the glass spewed across the bus.

The nightmare wasn't over.

Shore was still after them, and if he managed to injure the driver, then the bus would almost certainly crash. The crash alone might not be fatal, but it would leave them wide open for another attack.

"Don't stop," Brandon warned the driver, "and stay low in the seat."

The driver was cursing and praying at the same time. Brandon was mumbling something as well, but Willa didn't think she had the breath to utter anything.

Her baby began to kick, hard, but Willa welcomed the movement. It meant her daughter was safe. *For now.* But they weren't out of danger.

The next bullet proved that.

It came through the back window, tearing the glass apart, and it exited through the front. Thankfully, it didn't come near them or the driver, and the driver slammed on the accelerator to get them out of there.

"Shore's on foot," Brandon reminded her. "He won't be able to come after us for long."

Willa held her breath, waiting and trying to brace herself for more bullets. But the shots didn't continue.

Brandon lifted his head and looked out the window. "He's gone," he let her know.

Willa still didn't move. She lay there and prayed the threat was truly over.

"Drive to the nearest police station," Brandon told the driver, and he took out his phone.

While Brandon punched in some numbers, he helped her from the floor and moved her onto one of the seats. He dropped down onto the seat directly across from her.

"Are you okay?" he asked.

Willa nodded, but she doubted he believed her. For one thing, she was still breathing so fast that she was close to hyperventilating, and she was trembling from head to toe. It might be part of Brandon's job to be on the business end of gunfire, but until the hostage situation at the maternity hospital, Willa had never known what it was like to face real danger.

Well, now she knew.

And it couldn't continue.

Somehow, she had to find a safe place for her and her baby. If there was such a thing as a safe place. This was the third attack in four months. Four attacks if she counted being taken hostage at the hospital. Part of her was furious that time after time someone or something had endangered her precious baby. She wanted answers. She wanted justice.

But another part of her only wanted to run and hide.

Willa looked back at the broken glass and damage

the bullets had done to the seats. She also looked out at the sidewalk that was zipping by. No sign of Shore, thank God. Maybe they had finally lost him.

She listened while Brandon gave an update to whomever he had called. He also asked about Lieutenant Bo Duggan, and then about Martin Shore. Brandon's forehead bunched up when he apparently got a response.

"We're on our way," Brandon said to the person on the other end of the line, and he snapped his phone shut.

"They got Martin Shore?" she immediately asked.

He shook his head. "But they're looking. Backup arrived, and there are officers fanning out all over the area."

The hopeful tone was tinged with doubt. And Willa knew why. From what Brandon had told her, Martin Shore was a professional killer, and he probably knew how to evade the police. He was no doubt on the run so he could regroup.

And come after her again.

"Bo Duggan was shot," Brandon added, his voice practically a whisper. He closed his eyes a moment but not before she saw the flash of anger mixed with pain. "He's on the way to the hospital."

"I'm sorry." Not that it would probably help, but Willa reached out and touched his arm.

That touch brought his eyes open, and he met her gaze. "So am I. Sorry for the lieutenant and sorry that I didn't get to you sooner so I could stop this attack."

Willa didn't intend to take the blame for this, but it certainly wasn't Brandon's fault, either. The problem was she didn't know where to place the blame.

"You were trying to talk me into leaving with you and Lieutenant Duggan," she reminded him. She groaned softly. "And I was trying to figure out a way to escape."

He glanced back at the street and shook his head. "I wish to hell you had gotten out there before Shore arrived."

So had she. But here they were. Seconds after nearly being killed. Willa wondered if she would ever have peace of mind again, or if she would have to stay on the run for the rest of her life. It was possible that she could never give her precious baby a normal life.

"The police station's just around the block," the driver told them.

Willa had to take a deep breath. A police station filled with people she didn't trust. But she couldn't very well jump off the bus. Shore could still be out there. And besides, she didn't even have a house to return to. Other than the meager items in the messenger bag, the only things she had were Brandon and her memory.

Both were somewhat suspect.

"Don't trust the cops," Brandon mumbled, repeating what he'd seen on her computer screen and notes.

"Yes. But as you can see, I had my reasons for that distrust."

"And you still do?" he asked.

It wasn't a simple question, and there seemed to be a Texas-size amount of emotion behind it.

"I think I can trust you," she admitted. "Because I believe you truly are my baby's father."

Other than his word and the DNA results that could be fake, she had no other reason to believe him. But she did. Willa only hoped that didn't turn out to be another mistake.

The driver took a left turn and she spotted the police station just ahead.

Brandon put his hands on her shoulders and forced eye contact. "Look, when we get inside, I have no idea where they'll take us or what SAPD will tell you when they arrive."

That seemed like some kind of warning and Willa stared at him. "What do you mean?"

He opened his mouth. Closed it. Opened it again. Then, shook his head. He pulled her closer to him and put his mouth right against her ear.

"Shore was hired to kill you," Brandon whispered. "That part is the truth. So is the part about another hospital hostage situation." He paused. "But almost everything else that Bo and I told you is a lie."

It took a moment for that to sink in, but when it did, it felt like a punch. She gasped, a sound of outrage, and she tried to pull back, but Brandon held her in place.

The driver hit his brakes and brought the bus to a stop directly in front of police headquarters. Officers poured out from the building and began to run toward them.

"What do you mean everything else was a lie?" Willa demanded.

Brandon looked her straight in the eyes. "I'm not your ex-boyfriend, Willa. Before today, I'd never laid eyes or anything else on you."

BRANDON DIDN'T HAVE TIME to soothe that look in Willa's eyes. It was a mixture of anger, confusion and hurt. He also didn't have time to try to justify the lies he'd already told her.

Besides, there was no justification for that.

After SAPD had come to him and explained what was going on with a possible new hostage incident, Brandon had agreed to help them, but the plan had felt wrong from the very beginning.

And look where it'd gotten Willa.

She'd nearly been killed today, and they weren't out of the woods yet. As long as Shore was alive, the threat would be there.

"What do you mean you lied to me?" Willa demanded.

Brandon heard her, barely. That's because several officers ran onto the bus, and the sounds of their voices and footsteps drowned her out. One was plainclothes, in his late thirties with sandy-brown hair, and the other was younger and in a uniform. Both had their weapons drawn.

"I'm Sheriff Brandon Ruiz," he said, showing his badge. He slipped his gun back into his holster. "Any word about Lieutenant Duggan?"

The older officer shook his head. "Nothing yet."

Hell. Bo had to be all right. Brandon barely knew the man, but on the drive from San Antonio, Bo had talked all about his four-month-old twins. He'd also talked about his late wife, who'd died shortly after the maternity hostage incident. If something happened to Bo, those babies would be orphans.

Willa latched on to his arm when Brandon stood. "What do you mean you li—"

Brandon stopped that question by pressing his mouth

to hers. The kiss was hard, rough and way out of line, but he didn't want her to say anything in front of the other officers. He wasn't sure how much SAPD wanted him to explain about Willa and what might end up being a second hostage situation.

"We'll talk later," Brandon whispered and hoped his tone was enough of a warning for Willa to stay quiet.

He wouldn't blame her if she refused to cooperate, but he prayed that she would.

"Are you hurt?" the uniform asked them.

Brandon took the overnight bag from Willa and pulled her to her feet so he could check her out. She was riled to the core and confused, but she didn't appear to be injured physically. That was something at least.

"Do you need to see a doctor?" Brandon asked, and he held his breath hoping that she wasn't having contractions or anything.

"No," she answered through clenched teeth. "I only need to talk to you." Her gaze drifted to the police building, and she swallowed hard.

Don't trust the cops was probably racing through her head right now.

"SAPD is sending up some officers," the older cop relayed to Brandon. "They're already on their way. You can wait inside headquarters until they arrive. Plus, we'll need to get your statements on the shooting and the explosion."

"Ms. Marks will need a safe house right away," Brandon informed them. "After what she's been through, she needs to rest."

"I can find a place on my own," Willa insisted right back.

He didn't argue with her, for now, but there was no way he could let her go off on her own. God knows how he would be able to convince her of that, though.

Brandon led her off the bus, and the officers hurried them to the far side of the building to the patrol entrance, probably because they were still concerned about Shore being at large.

"I'd like to go someplace private," Willa told the officer the moment they were inside. "Because Sheriff Ruiz and I need to talk. It's important, and it can't wait."

The officer volleyed glances between Brandon and her, and the man was no doubt wondering what this was all about. Brandon didn't intend to fill him in, at least not until he'd spoken with the officers from SAPD. Even if those officers had indeed already left their headquarters, they probably wouldn't arrive for at least another forty-five minutes.

"Follow me," the officer finally said. He took them through the maze of squad rooms and stopped outside a break room that had chairs, a sofa and some vending machines. "I hope this'll do," the officer commented. "And while you're talking I'll see about an update on Lieutenant Duggan."

Brandon thanked the man but didn't say anything else until he was out of earshot. Too bad there was no door so he could give them an extra layer of privacy.

They were going to need it.

"Why did you lie?" Willa demanded.

Since this probably wouldn't be a short or quiet conversation, Brandon placed her overnight bag on the floor and pulled her to the side of a vending machine.

"Because SAPD convinced me that the fastest way to stop another hostage incident was to get you to trust me."

Her eyes narrowed, but it didn't seem to be simply from anger. "And it worked. Well, partly. I *was* starting to trust you."

"You still can," he promised.

She looked at him as if he'd lost his mind. "You're a liar."

"About some things. It's true, I'd never met you before today." It was a risk because she might slap him, but Brandon placed his hand over her stomach. "But I really am your baby's father."

She blinked and then stared at him, examining his eyes. "You expect me to believe that?"

"It's the truth." And he blew out a long breath. It was actually a relief to tell her the truth. "Nearly ten years ago I was in the military and headed to a dangerous assignment in the Middle East. I was engaged at the time, and my then fiancée convinced me to store some semen in case I was injured. When I got back from the assignment, the engagement was over. And I knew I didn't need what I'd stored, so I signed a donor agreement, and it was sent to a sperm bank."

Willa continued to study him and was no doubt trying to decide if he was telling the truth.

"A sperm bank?" she questioned.

He nodded. "Obviously it was the one you used for your artificial insemination."

"Obviously." But there was still a lot of skepticism in her voice. "Why should I believe you?"

"Because it's true. The DNA test results I gave you

are real," he continued. "And it proves I'm the baby's biological father."

Brandon tried not to show what he was feeling. He didn't want Willa to mistake it for dishonesty. But that last word, *father,* had not come easily.

And probably never would.

He kept that to himself.

The staring went on, and on, and finally Willa's shoulders relaxed. A weary breath left her mouth, and she sagged against the wall.

Since she looked ready to drop, Brandon held on to her. Or rather he tried. But Willa pushed him away.

"My sperm donor," she mumbled. She shook her head. "How did SAPD find you?"

"Bo Duggan said they'd been looking at all the angles as to how to approach you, so they kept digging into your background. You aren't close to anyone in your family, so they widened the search. And finally got to your medical records. They traced the donor number for your insemination, and that led them to me."

"They knew you were a cop?" she asked.

"Not at first. But I think that ended up being a bonus for them." It had certainly given the police captain carte blanche to press him into cooperating. "SAPD knew you wouldn't welcome them with open arms, and they were desperate. They need your cooperation."

"They need me to remember," Willa corrected. "To remember what happened during the hostage situation so I can see if it relates to what might happen in another crisis. But I can't remember. I've tried and I can't."

He lifted his shoulder. "That's where I was supposed to come in. They want me to coax you into going through more therapy. You've already made so much progress. You said yourself that your short-term memory problems were over."

"I lied." She huffed and pushed her hair away from her face.

Brandon had to do a double take. "What?"

Willa dodged his gaze. "My memory's not nearly as bad as it was right after my injury, but sometimes I still forget. That's why I put your picture on my PDA." Her gaze snapped back to him and she scowled. "I typed in my PDA that I thought I could trust you. I need to change that."

"No. You don't."

Her scowl melted away, and tears sprang to her eyes. That's when Brandon noticed that she was still trembling. From the attack, no doubt.

Even though it was a risk on many levels, he pulled her to him. Willa fought him, struggling to break the embrace, but Brandon held on.

"That's my baby you're carrying," he reminded her. And in doing so, he reminded himself. "I'm not going to let you go through this alone."

Willa likely had no clue as to what it took for him to say that. She pulled back slightly and, even though she was still blinking away tears, she looked up at him. Her breath broke and she melted against him.

"Nothing bad can happen to this baby," she muttered through the sobs.

"It won't." Though it was a promise that would be hell to keep.

He touched his mouth to her forehead. Just a touch. But he felt the heat spear through him. Brandon definitely didn't want to feel that heat, but he couldn't deny it was there.

What the hell was wrong with him?

He wanted to believe the attraction existed because of the baby. Maybe some kind of primal DNA trigger so he'd feel compelled to protect the unborn child.

Brandon silently cursed.

This attraction didn't have anything to do with the baby. He was attracted to Willa. Plain and simple. And that attraction could cause some big-time problems for both of them.

Thankfully, his phone rang because Brandon was ready for both a distraction and news. After he glanced at his caller ID, he figured he would at least get the latter.

The call was from Sergeant Cash Newsome, a cop in SAPD and someone Brandon had known for years. They'd both been in the army together and had done a tour of duty in the Middle East. Since Cash was also Bo Duggan's right-hand man, Brandon hoped he would have an update about the lieutenant's status.

"I heard you ran into Martin Shore," Cash greeted.

"Literally," Brandon confirmed. "How's Bo?"

"It's good news. He has a non-life-threatening gunshot wound to the shoulder. He'll be out of commission for a day or two, but he'll make a full recovery."

Brandon released the breath he'd been holding. "And what about Martin Shore?"

"Still no sign of him. We haven't given up," Cash quickly added. "We're searching the area, going door to door. We won't stop looking until we find him."

They might get lucky, but Brandon had to be realistic.

A hired gun that was gutsy enough to attack in a residential neighborhood in broad daylight probably had made arrangements for an escape. Shore was likely already out of the area.

And planning round two.

"Any idea why Shore came after Willa earlier than intel had indicated?" Brandon asked.

"Our best guess is that he had her house under surveillance and saw Bo and you arrive. He probably thought he should go ahead while he still had her in his sights."

That made sense, and it told him a lot about Shore. The man could and would improvise, and that made him even more dangerous.

"We've arranged a safe house for Willa," Cash continued. "It's local so you won't have to be on the road too long with her. I guess it goes without saying that she'll be in your protective custody."

Yeah. Without saying. Brandon was too deep into this to turn back now.

"Sergeant Harris McCoy and I will be there in about a half hour, and we'll take you to the safe house." Cash paused. "We'd also like Willa to see a therapist who specializes in recovering lost memories."

Brandon glanced at Willa. Even though she probably hadn't heard what Cash had just said, she could no doubt sense Brandon's own hesitation. He was hesitating not because he thought the therapist was a bad idea but because he wasn't sure he'd be able to convince Willa to trust anyone associated with the police.

Including him.

"I'll have to get back to you on that last part," Brandon told Cash.

Willa's left eyebrow lifted.

"Why?" Cash asked. "Have you talked her into co-operating yet?"

"No."

"Try harder. Because we've just gotten an update on what could be our next hostage situation."

"And?" Brandon asked when Cash didn't continue.

"And the news isn't good."

Chapter Six

Two days.

The short timeline kept going through Willa's head, stuck like a broken record, on the entire drive from Austin to the safe house. Two days.

Christmas.

That's when SAPD thought there'd be another hostage situation at a hospital. Or at least that's the information Sergeant Cash Newsome had relayed to Brandon while they were waiting in the break room at the Austin P.D. building. The authorities had two days to stop another nightmare from happening. But while the so-called intel had provided a time, SAPD didn't have a location. Or a motive.

They were counting on Willa to help them.

"Good luck with that," she said to herself. She huffed at that and the so-called safe house as it came into view.

Even if she could completely regain her memory before then, Willa wasn't convinced she actually knew anything that would help.

Two days.

And God knew how many women and babies would

have to go through the same kind of hell that she'd gone through for the past four months.

"You okay?" Brandon asked, bringing the car to a stop in the tiny garage of the safe house.

Willa considered lying but decided it was useless. "No."

He matched her heavy sigh with one of his own and hit the button on the automatic garage opener. He waited until the garage door was completely shut before they got out of the nondescript dark blue car that SAPD had provided.

There was a single light on in the laundry room situated just off the garage entrance, but there was enough moonlight filtering through the windows that she didn't have any trouble seeing.

Willa glanced around at the safe house. Well, what there was of it anyway.

It was small, much like her rental place that Shore had blown up on the other side of town. Except this place wasn't in the suburbs. It was in the country, halfway between San Antonio and Austin, and to get to it they'd used a rural road. Their nearest neighbor was more than a mile away.

She walked through the house, taking inventory. Two sparsely decorated bedrooms, one bath and a living-dining-kitchen combo. Though Brandon and she had already eaten dinner at police headquarters, the fridge had been stocked with plastic-wrapped sandwiches, bottled water and juice.

The cramped quarters and limited food options, however, meant nothing to her. The only thing Willa cared about right now was being as far away from Martin Shore as possible.

She watched as Brandon double-locked the door, and then he took out the codes that Sergeant Cash Newsome had given him so he could arm the security system.

"I suppose the windows and both the front and back doors are connected to the system?" she asked.

He nodded. "They are. There's also an alarm that runs around the immediate perimeter of the house in case anyone attempts a break-in. It's supposed to be safe."

She nodded as well. Then swallowed hard. Because no place might be safe enough to protect them from Martin Shore. Or the people who might be planning another hostage situation.

Brandon turned slowly and faced her. "I don't want us to sleep here inside the house."

Willa had thought he was about to tell her to get some rest. Maybe even give her another reassurance that nothing else bad would happen. She hadn't expected that from him. And her breath stalled in her throat.

"Do you trust me?" he asked.

The question hit her almost as hard as his bombshell about not wanting to stay there. She automatically reached for the PDA in her bag. But Willa didn't need to see his picture or the note she'd written to go along with it.

She remembered.

And what she remembered was that she *thought* she could trust him.

"What's this about?" she wanted to know.

Brandon scrubbed his hand over his face. "You know I made several calls after I got off the phone with Sergeant Cash Newsome?"

Yes. He'd stepped to the other side of the room for those calls, and he'd whispered so she couldn't hear. Willa figured he was discussing the therapy appointment that SAPD had made for her. An appointment that was supposed to happen at eight the following morning. Since it was already nine in the evening, that appointment wasn't far off.

"Cash is an old army buddy, and while I trust him, I wanted someone outside of SAPD," Brandon explained. "I contacted another old friend who runs a security company."

"Is that the person who dropped you off the duffel bag?" she asked.

"Yeah." Brandon had that particular bag slung over his shoulder, but he eased it off and set it on an overstuffed fabric chair. "I asked him to bring me some supplies that I might need. I also asked him to see if he's heard anything about a possible leak at SAPD."

Her breath stalled again. Mercy, she hadn't braced herself nearly enough for any of this. "What kind of leak?"

"The worst kind for us. A leak in communication. I don't like the fact that SAPD's intel told them that Shore wouldn't attack you until tonight."

She thought about that a moment, and the conclusion she came to caused her heart rate to spike. "You think someone tipped Shore off?"

Brandon shrugged. "I don't want to believe it, but I

also don't want to put blind trust in people I don't really know."

Neither did she. "You don't think Bo Duggan could have done this?"

"Not him. But I don't know how many people in SAPD had access to the information about Shore." He made a sweeping glance around the room. "Or this place."

That didn't steady her heart. Willa slid her hand over her stomach. "So, what should we do?"

Brandon didn't answer immediately, and his forehead bunched up. "My friend sent me several portable security cameras and a monitor. I want to set the cameras up here, inside, but I want us to sleep in the car in the garage."

She instantly thought of the grenade that Shore had tossed into her rental. "Shore could try to blow us up again."

Brandon nodded. "He could. But I'll keep watch on the monitor. And the cameras are motion-activated and will sound if they're triggered. If anyone approaches the house, I can drive us out of here." He reached out, touched her arm and rubbed gently. "This is just a precaution, Willa."

He added the last part as if he expected her to challenge him, but Willa had no intentions of doing that.

She nodded. "I need to go to the bathroom, but once you have the camera set up, we can go back to the car."

It wouldn't be comfortable, but she still might be able to sleep there. Her fatigue was past the bone-weary stage, and she had no choice but to rest.

Willa took her toiletries from her bag so she could brush her teeth and take her prenatal vitamin. She also used the bathroom and hoped she wouldn't have to make too many treks back into the house because of her pregnancy bladder.

When she came back into the living room, Brandon had lowered all the blinds in the house and was setting up the tiny golf-ball-size camera in the front window. Since it was so small and white, it blended right into the window sill.

"There's a camera in the kitchen," he explained, "and the front bedroom. I'll put the other one just outside the garage door, and then I can monitor all of them with that." He pointed to a GPS-looking device with four split screens.

"We can take turns watching it," she suggested.

"No need. The monitor will beep if any of the cameras are triggered by motion. That means you can get some sleep. Think of the baby," he added before Willa could argue.

"I do, all the time," she mumbled. "Do you?" She instantly regretted that question. Brandon had only recently found out he was going to be a father, and he probably hadn't even come to terms with it yet. Added to that, he had the extra worry about keeping them safe.

Willa waved off the question and reached for her bag.

"I think about the baby," he said, his words soft and slow. He took the bag from her, keeping his attention focused on it and not her.

"It's okay," she assured him. "When the danger has

passed, I don't expect anything from you. In fact, I don't want anything from you."

That was a semi-truth. Her body wanted him. For sex. How ironic. She hadn't had as much of a sexual twinge since she'd gotten pregnant; yet near Brandon, in her last trimester no less, she kept feeling that tug deep within her.

"Good." And that was all he said for several moments. "Honestly, I'm not sure I can give you and this baby what you really need."

His eyes met hers for just a second, before he looked away and put the monitor in the equipment bag. He hoisted it over his other shoulder and headed for the garage door. Willa grabbed the pillow and cover that had been stacked on the sofa and followed him.

This was good, she assured herself. Brandon didn't want to be part of her or their baby's life. That's exactly the way she'd planned things. Heck, it was the reason she'd no doubt used artificial insemination. Because she hadn't wanted a man in her life.

So, why did his confession sting?

She barely knew the man and, other than the fact he was almost certainly the biological father of her baby, that was the only thing that connected them.

Well, except for the attraction.

And the danger.

And this entire bizarre connection she felt with him.

Willa huffed. She was talking herself into falling hard for Brandon, and that could be a fatal mistake.

Since the front seats of the car reclined, Willa got in on the passenger's side and prepared a makeshift bed.

Brandon eased the garage door open just a fraction and placed the camera outside. After closing it, he got behind the wheel and started his own preparations. Not for a bed, though, but for security. So that he wouldn't lose them, he put the keys in the ignition, set up the monitor on the dashboard and placed the bags on the backseat.

Willa turned, leaned over and retrieved the PDA from her bag. What she hadn't counted on was Brandon moving at the same time. He turned to adjust his holster, and they practically collided.

And then they froze.

Breath met breath, and Willa got an instant reminder of that attraction. It suddenly raced through her. Hot and wild. As if her huge pregnant belly wasn't a hindrance to anything sexual.

Brandon made a sound, deep within his throat. A sort of rumbling. That sound stirred through her as well. So did his scent. Something manly and woodsy. That scent alerted every part of her body that hadn't already been alerted.

"This can't happen," she whispered.

"Yeah."

But the single word had hardly left his mouth when he dragged her to him and put his lips on hers. His scent had caused a jolt, but the kiss created an avalanche.

Willa found herself sliding her arms around him and pulling him closer. She found herself deepening the kiss. And she found herself getting lost in the steamy maze of passion she immediately knew she couldn't control. She was on fire, and her body was urging her to keep pulling him closer, to keep kissing him, to continue this insanity no matter the cost.

If she'd thought his scent had her hormonal number, his taste was even more potent. That taste drew her in. And so did Brandon's embrace. His kiss was gentle and left her with no doubts that it was exactly what she wanted.

But shouldn't have.

Willa latched on to that thought and kept mentally repeating it. However, she wasn't the one to stop the kiss. It was Brandon. He eased her away from him and glanced at the monitor.

"I have to keep you safe," he said with a lot of regret and heavy breath in his voice.

Since safety was the main reason they were here in the car, Willa had no comeback for that. He did need to keep an eye on the monitor. He needed to protect her because that was the only way to keep her baby safe. Still, it was a battle to get herself to move away from him.

Willa settled into the seat and tried to level her breathing. Her body was still on fire, but her brain just kept reminding her that she had done the right thing by stopping the makeout session—even if it felt wrong.

"Are you sure we weren't lovers?" she asked, trying to keep things light.

"I'm sure." There was no lightness in his voice. It was strained, just like his expression. The need was still in his intense brown eyes. But the corner of his mouth lifted. "Trust me, I would have remembered having sex with you."

Yes. And even with her amnesia, Willa thought she

might have remembered, too. Brandon had a unique way of being unforgettable.

Well, maybe.

She glanced down at the PDA cupped in her hand and scrolled through the photos and information she'd stored there. She remembered everything she'd recorded for the past two weeks. Prior to that, her memory was spotty and prior to that, there were huge gaps. Two weeks wasn't nearly enough time for her to trust herself. So, Willa began making notes. About the attack from Martin Shore. About Brandon.

About everything.

She had to get everything down before she fell asleep, and that wouldn't be long. Despite the fiery kiss and Brandon's closeness, her body would soon have to rest.

"The night can be the worst time for me," she explained to Brandon as she continued to type. "Sometimes, when I wake up, everything in my memory is gone."

And she meant *everything*.

He stayed quiet a moment. "What should I do if that happens?"

"Run," she joked. But then she shook her head. "I'll be confused. I might even try to attack you because I won't know who you are. But just remind me that your picture is in here." She tapped her PDA.

Brandon looked at it, then at her. His gaze lingered a moment on her face, and on a heavy breath, he turned back to the monitor.

"Sleep," he insisted.

She nodded but didn't close her eyes. Willa pulled

the covers to her chin, snuggling them around her so she'd stay warm, but she fastened her attention to the monitor. Thanks to the four cameras, every angle of the house and attached garage were covered. Even in the darkness, they would be able to see someone approaching.

Hopefully, it would stay that way, but Willa had a bad feeling that things were about to get a whole lot worse.

BRANDON POPPED ANOTHER mint in his mouth and wished it were a big gulp of strong coffee. He needed a hit of caffeine badly, but he didn't want to go back inside the house to see if there was any. That would mean either waking Willa or leaving her alone.

He had no plans to do either.

Since the monitor for the security cameras would alert him to any movement around the house, Brandon had managed a couple of catnaps, but with each one, the nightmares had come.

He glanced at Willa who was sleeping soundly in the reclined seat. The covers had shifted, draping down below her left breast. Brandon eased the cover back in place. He noticed her PDA then. It had slipped from her hand and was now on the console between them.

Was there something stored in the PDA that would help the cops stop another hostage situation? Maybe. Maybe it also contained something that would help Willa restore her memory. At least that was the justification he used when he read the first page entry.

Your name is Willa Marks, and you have amnesia and post-concussional neurosis, also called short-term memory loss. Everything you need to know is on this PDA.

There was a list of places where she had cash stored and her doctor's phone number, followed by a list of rules. Well, two rules to be specific.

Number one: don't trust the cops.
Number two: stay in hiding.

Neither was a surprise. Twice Willa had nearly been killed when she'd trusted the cops. If their positions had been reversed, he might have written the same damn memos.

He scrolled down farther to the next entry that Willa had labeled Latest Update.

The man beside me is Sheriff Brandon Ruiz. My baby's father. Use caution. He has secrets.

"Secrets?" he mumbled. Yeah, he had them.

Well, one anyway. But it was a secret that could affect everything.

What the hell was he going to do about Willa and the baby?

She needed help, all right. But she needed someone with less emotional baggage than he had. He certainly didn't fit the bill.

Frustrated with that and the lack of news about the case, Brandon took out his phone and sent a text message to Cash to see if there was an update. The moment he hit the send button, he heard the beep. It was so soft that it was barely audible, but it went through him as if it'd been a shout.

Brandon's gaze flew to the monitor. He checked the feed from all the cameras and didn't see anything out of the ordinary. Well, not at first anyway. He moved closer to the screen, trying to pick through the pitchy darkness of the tiny images.

There.

Beneath the bedroom window.

He spotted the man dressed head to toe in black. His movement had obviously triggered the perimeter security sensor. Brandon watched as the man lifted his hand and bashed something against the glass in the window.

"Willa," Brandon whispered. "We have to get out of here now."

Her eyes flew open, and she gave the seat a quick adjustment so she was in a sitting position. Her attention went straight to the monitor.

"Is it Shore?" she asked.

"I can't tell." But Brandon would put money on the fact that it was the assassin. If not, then it was someone equally dangerous.

"Put on your seat belt," Brandon instructed. He did the same. "And stay down. The second I open the garage door, I'm driving out of here fast."

That was a risk, of course, because Shore could shoot at them, but Brandon knew that was a risk he had to take—especially when he saw the man toss something through the broken bedroom window.

Hell.

It could be another grenade. And if it was, the

explosion could easily destroy the garage, or at minimum, the damage from a blast could trap them inside.

Brandon started the car and hit the remote opener clipped to the visor. It seemed to take way too long for the door to lift, and with each passing second, he prayed that Shore wouldn't have time to make it to the front of the garage entrance so he could shoot at them head-on.

As soon as Brandon had clearance to get out of the garage, he jammed his foot on the accelerator, and the car bolted out into the darkness.

The shot came almost immediately and shattered the back windshield.

"Stay down!" he reminded Willa, though he knew that might not be enough. Bullets could go through seats as easily as they could through glass.

The sound of the second shot drowned out his repeated warning for her to stay down. The bullet tore through what was left of the safety glass, and the shooter quickly followed it up with a third and fourth shot. But that wasn't all. Behind them, there was an explosion, and both the house and the garage burst into fireballs.

Brandon didn't dare risk looking at Willa to make sure she was okay because he had to focus on getting them away from the shooter.

He headed for the road and glanced in the side mirror to see if the gunman was in pursuit. It was impossible to tell, but it was obvious the guy was still in shooting range because yet another bullet tore through the side of the car. Thank God the shots missed the tires or their chances of escape would drop significantly.

The shots stopped, and Brandon continued to tear his way down the country road. He had to slow down to take a sharp curve, but as soon as he could, he sped up again.

He saw the headlights then.

They flared on behind them, and even though Brandon couldn't see their attacker, he figured the guy had hidden his vehicle nearby. He'd probably killed the car lights so that they wouldn't be alerted. The plan might have worked, too, if Brandon hadn't suspected there might be an attack and set up those security cameras.

Beside him, he could hear Willa's heavy breathing, and from the corner of his eye, he could see that she had her hands splayed protectively over her belly.

"He's following us, isn't he?" she asked. Her voice was raspy and thick.

Brandon glanced in the side mirror and saw the headlights. The guy was definitely in pursuit. "Yeah," he confirmed. "Hang on."

He took the next turn faster than he should have, and Brandon fought with the steering wheel to keep his vehicle on the road. He hated putting Willa through this, but there was no other choice. With Willa in the car, he couldn't risk stopping to have a showdown with this SOB. Later though, he hoped he got the chance to beat this guy to dust.

The anger roared through Brandon, and he could feel the dangerous energy course in his blood. With it, came the flashbacks. Like the nightmares, they were always there, ready to rear their ugly heads. He pinned his attention to the road, to the curves, and forced the old demons to remain at bay.

"Where are we going?" she asked. She levered herself up just a fraction to check her side mirror, but Brandon caught onto her shoulder and shoved her back down.

"Once we get to the highway, I'll drive toward San Antonio. Maybe I can lose him on the interstate and if not, maybe the traffic will get him to back off."

Both possibilities were long shots, but they were the only shots that Brandon had.

"Should I call 9-1-1?" Willa asked. But she hadn't said it eagerly, more as a last resort.

It was a last resort they couldn't risk.

"No," he answered. He could have sworn he heard her sigh with relief.

He took another curve, then another, but the vehicle stayed behind them. Too close. And worse, it was gaining. The only good thing about their situation was that the driver wouldn't be able to fire at them while trying to maintain the speed. Still, that didn't mean they were safe.

Brandon reached a straight stretch of the road and was able to go faster. So did the other car, and it closed in. The driver had on his high beams, making it hard for Brandon to see, but he could tell the vehicle was an SUV. It was much larger and faster than the car he was driving, so the SUV quickly ate up the distance between them.

"Hold on," Brandon warned Willa.

Just as the SUV smashed into their rear bumper.

Brandon fought to keep the car on the road, and he

didn't let up on the accelerator. He continued to race toward the highway. If his calculations were correct, that was less than a mile away.

The SUV rammed into them again, and the jolt sent them both snapping in their seats. He bit back some profanity and prayed all this jostling around wouldn't hurt the baby or Willa. While he was praying, he added that he could get them safely out of there.

There was another sharp curve, and then the road stretched out again in a straight line. The SUV's driver took advantage of it and slammed into the back of their car again. Brandon kept a tight grip on the steering wheel, somehow managing to keep the car on the road.

Finally, he spotted the highway, and Brandon took the turn on what had to be two wheels. He quickly righted the car and took off.

Despite the late hour, it wasn't long before he spotted another vehicle just ahead of them. Brandon raced toward it and hoped there would be others to deter the SUV driver from another attack.

The SUV stayed close, and Brandon braced himself in case they were rammed again, but the guy stayed back.

Brandon passed the other vehicle but then slowed, hoping to keep the car between them and the SUV.

"Are we losing him?" Willa asked.

"Not just yet."

There were several other vehicles just ahead on the highway, and Brandon got as close to them as possible. The seconds clicked off in his head, and he held his breath until he saw the cluster of lit buildings at an exit.

He wouldn't leave the highway just yet, but only a few miles ahead was the exit for the county sheriff's office and the fire department. He would get off the highway there and, if necessary, he'd even pull into the sheriff's parking lot.

Willa sat up just a fraction and glanced in the side mirror. She stared back at the SUV that was now several cars behind them. "Shore came out into the open at the rental house so he could follow us," she reminded him. "Neither the neighborhood street nor the traffic stopped him."

Yeah. Brandon was aware of that. And that was one of the reasons the knot in his gut had tightened to the point of being painful. If that was Shore in the SUV, then why had he backed off? Of course, the answer might be that it wasn't Shore.

That thought caused Brandon to take a deep breath.

Willa shook her head. "I'm past being tired of this. All I want is for my baby to be safe."

Brandon wanted the same thing, but he was aware that the danger was far from being over.

He put on his blinker when he reached the exit for the sheriff's office, and when Willa saw where he was headed, she sat up even farther in her seat.

"I thought you didn't want to involve the cops," she questioned.

"I don't. We can't," he corrected a moment later. He pulled into the well-lit parking lot and stopped in the spot that was closest to the front door.

The SUV slowed to a crawl but didn't turn into the lot. Brandon watched as it crept out of sight.

The driver wouldn't go far. No. He would wait for them to make a move. For now, the only move Brandon intended to do was stay put. He could go into the sheriff's office, of course, as a final resort, but the sheriff would almost certainly contact the San Antonio Police.

He kept watch to make sure the SUV didn't circle back around, and he glanced at Willa to check that she was all right. She wasn't. She was pale and trembling.

Brandon put his arm around her and eased her closer. She welcomed the contact.

He tried to figure out how to word what he had to tell her and decided there was no easy way to spell out their situation. Basically, they were in the worst kind of trouble, and Willa needed to know that.

"Shore—or whoever just attacked us—had to have known how to find us," Brandon explained.

She pulled back, met his gaze. "This means there's a leak?"

He nodded and hated the fear he saw in her eyes. "You were right, Willa. We can't trust the cops."

She made a sound of agreement and blinked back tears. "What about Sergeant Cash Newsome? Can you call him?"

"Maybe." Brandon did trust his old friend and would try to contact him but not now. Not until he could figure out a way to make sure any conversation he had with Cash would be private.

"So what do we do?" Willa asked.

Chapter Seven

The sound of someone talking woke her.

Willa forced open her heavy eyelids and realized it was no longer dark, and they were no longer parked outside the sheriff's office. The car was moving. And judging from the massive buildings around them, they were driving through downtown San Antonio.

She sat up, yawned and looked at the man behind the wheel. She recognized that dark hair and those steamy brown eyes.

"I remember you," she mumbled.

With the phone sandwiched between his shoulder and ear, Brandon glanced at her and nodded. The corner of his mouth lifted into a near smile. Thank God she didn't have to re-create her life and memories this morning. But then Willa remembered something else.

The danger.

That kicked up her heartbeat to an uncomfortable level, and she looked all around them to make certain Shore wasn't still following them. There were plenty of vehicles on the road, but she saw no signs of that SUV.

"We'll be there in a few minutes," Brandon told the person on the other end of the line. "Remember, this stays just between us."

He closed his phone and shoved it back into his pocket. "That was Cash."

Her breath went thin. "You're sure we can trust him?"

"He's given me no reason not to. Not yet anyway," Brandon added in a mumble. "Cash insists there isn't a leak at SAPD. He thinks Shore is tracking us some other way."

"How?"

"Well, it's not my cell phone because I know it has an anti-tracking device." Brandon glanced at her PDA. And her stomach knotted. It was her lifeline. Her security blanket. It had saved her life—literally.

"It's just a possibility," he added.

True, but Shore was finding them somehow, and maybe her PDA had some kind of GPS tracking system.

It made her physically ill to think of what she had to do, but she couldn't let her lifeline put her baby at risk. Willa opened the glove compartment and fished out a pen.

"Don't give me any reason to regret this," she warned Brandon, and Willa waited until he made eye contact with her before she scrawled the words across her palm.

Trust Brandon Ruiz.

He glanced at the sentence and then mumbled some profanity. Profanity he didn't explain as he brought the car to a stop in a hotel parking lot.

"Leave the PDA in the car," he told her and checked their surroundings. "We won't be coming back to this vehicle or the parking lot."

She glanced around as well, and her attention landed on the hotel. "Are we staying here?"

Brandon shook his head, grabbed her overnight bag and opened the door. "In and out. We'll be on foot for a few blocks."

Good. She didn't want to be anywhere near her PDA or the vehicle with the shot-out windows. "But I'll need to find a bathroom soon," she let him know.

Brandon took her request to heart and hurried them from the car into the hotel. They didn't stop in the lobby but went to the back and exited into another parking lot. They walked past two more buildings before entering another hotel. Willa expected them to exit this one as well, but she came to a dead stop when she spotted the sandy-haired man in the lobby.

He was almost certainly a cop.

Willa didn't know who he was, but he did seem familiar. About six feet tall, lanky build and green eyes. Cop's eyes.

Brandon stopped directly in front of the man. "Willa, this is Sergeant Cash Newsome."

She still didn't release the breath she was holding.

Brandon leaned closer to Cash and lowered his voice to a whisper. "If this puts Willa in any more danger, you'll be the one to answer for it."

Cash stiffened, and his friendly expression faded. "That doesn't sound like something an old friend would say."

Brandon scowled. "Friendship only gets you one

shot. If Shore finds us here, then I'm taking Willa into deep hiding where SAPD and their possible leak can't ever find her."

"Think of those women who could become the next hostages," Cash countered.

"I'm thinking of Willa and the baby. Right now, they come first."

That started a staring match between the two men, and Cash hitched his shoulder toward the elevator. He started in that direction. So did Brandon. Willa stayed put, but after glancing down at what she'd written on her hand, she cursed and caught up to the men.

They went to the fifth floor, and Cash directed them into a suite that was nearly the same size as the safe house they'd left hours earlier. There were massive windows revealing the city's skyline, but what snagged Willa's attention was the smell of bacon and eggs that was coming from the silver dome-covered plates on the coffee table. Her stomach growled, and the baby kicked as if sensing it was time to eat as well.

Brandon handed her the bag. "Go ahead to the bathroom and then I'll explain what's going on after you've had some breakfast."

She really did need to use the bathroom, but she didn't budge. "I'd like to hear now."

Cash and Brandon exchanged glances. Cash's expression was laced with skepticism, but Brandon looked as if he were bracing himself for an argument.

"We need your help," Cash insisted.

But she ignored him and stared at Brandon instead. "What do they want you to convince me to do?"

"They want you to see a doctor who might be able to help you recover your memory."

"A psychiatrist who's a friend of mine," Cash supplied. "Her name is Dr. Lenora Farris and she'll be here in about twenty minutes."

"A shrink?" Willa made sure she let her tone convey her displeasure, and she aimed that displeasure at Brandon. "I've already seen therapists."

"She's supposedly different." Brandon turned so that he was between Cash and her. "I thought if you could remember it might help us put an end to the danger. *All* the danger for both you and any other possible hostages. We might also be able to figure out who hired Shore to come after you."

Willa couldn't argue with that, but she still wasn't convinced this would help. Plus, they were in a hotel suite with a cop, and if there was a leak, they could be sitting ducks for another attack.

Brandon put his mouth right against her ear. "I agreed to two hours. That's it. And then we're getting out of here."

Willa still wanted to argue, but then Brandon brushed a kiss on her forehead. That took the fight right out of her. Of course, maybe the fatigue and her full bladder were partly responsible as well. She shifted the bag to her shoulder, huffed and headed for the adjoining bathroom.

She didn't dawdle, but she did take the time to freshen up and change her top. Thankfully, she'd packed a green sweater in her overnight bag.

When she went back into the main room of the suite, it was obvious she was interrupting a tense discussion—maybe even an argument. Whatever had been going on came to an abrupt halt when Cash and Brandon spotted her.

Brandon scrubbed his hand over his face. "Eat," he told Willa. And he headed to the bathroom, leaving her alone with Cash.

Since her stomach was still growling and she was getting light-headed, Willa sat and helped herself to one of the plates. There was even a glass of milk and a bottle of prenatal vitamins on the tray.

"You don't remember me?" Cash asked. He poured himself a cup of coffee from a gleaming silver carafe and took the chair across from her.

"No. We've met?"

He nodded. "I was the first officer to get to you after the hostage standoff ended."

Without her PDA, she couldn't confirm that, so Willa settled for making a noncommittal sound while she ate her scrambled eggs.

"I found you in the hall outside the hospital lab," he continued. "You'd fallen, or something. You were barely conscious."

That got her attention. Had she known that "barely conscious" part? She didn't think so. Willa was sure she had put in her notes that she regained consciousness not at the maternity hospital but in the medical center after she came out of a coma.

"Did I say anything when you found me?" she asked.

He shrugged. "You were worried about losing the baby."

Well, that was a no-brainer, but she got the feeling

that Cash was withholding something. Or maybe it was just her overactive imagination.

Brandon came out of the bathroom at the same moment there was a knock at the door. The sound sent both men reaching for their weapons, and it was Brandon who went to the door to peek out the viewer.

"It's a woman," he relayed to Cash. "Tall with auburn hair."

"Dr. Farris," Cash supplied. He confirmed that by looking through the viewer as well, and then opened the door to greet their visitor.

Since she wasn't always able to rely on her memory, Willa had gotten accustomed to reading people. There was usually something—a quick unguarded glance, a tightening of the mouth. Some small detail.

But not with Dr. Farris.

Cash made the introductions, but Willa still didn't get any clues when she shook the woman's hand. Dr. Farris seemed friendly enough but, more than anything, she was a blank slate. Maybe because of her psychiatric training.

"Willa," the doctor greeted, and she held on to Willa's hand for several seconds. "I'm here to help you."

Willa didn't try to hide her skepticism. "Others have tried. And failed."

The doctor nodded and calmly whisked a loose curl from her pale ivory face. "But those therapies were used early on after your injury. Sergeant Newsome tells me you've made improvements since then and that you're not having as many issues with your short-term memory."

Willa aimed a scowl at Cash. "And how exactly would you know that?"

Cash shrugged his shoulders. "Lieutenant Bo Duggan. I had a long talk with him before I set all of this up."

Then obviously the lieutenant was recovering. That was something at least, especially since he'd gotten shot while trying to protect her.

Brandon stepped even closer to Willa and caught her hand in his. However, he directed his attention to Dr. Farris. "How do you think you can help Willa?"

"Well, since we obviously can't use any drugs to induce an altered state, I want to use something called Neuro-Linguistic Programming—NLP—that incorporates video hypnosis. I plan to use triggers that might cue in other parts of her brain to unlock the lost memories."

"What kind of triggers?" Willa demanded.

The doctor offered her a calm smile. "Both visual and auditory. By using NLP, I want to re-create the environment of the maternity ward the way it was when the hostage situation started."

Willa felt a chill go over her. "I'm not going back to that hospital."

"You don't have to. In a way, I'm bringing the hospital to you." Dr. Farris extracted a shiny DVD from her purse. "My assistants and I have worked on this for hours so you can replicate the experience."

Willa didn't want to replicate it because her time as a hostage had almost certainly been terrifying. But she couldn't refuse the opportunity to regain her memory simply because she was scared. As Brandon had already pointed out, the information trapped in her mind could ultimately give them the name of the person trying to kill them and it could save those possible Christmas hostages.

"Is this safe?" Brandon asked.

"Absolutely." The doctor didn't hesitate, either. "And if Willa becomes agitated, I'll stop." She looked at Willa then and waited.

Willa went over everything the doctor had just told her. This, whatever this was, wouldn't harm the baby. And she could stop if it got too extreme. There was no way she could refuse, not with her risking so little and with so much at stake for the future hostages.

Willa finally nodded.

Dr. Farris didn't give a sigh of relief. She didn't show any emotion as she went to the large flat-screen TV and inserted the disk in the DVD player.

"You two should wait in the other room," the doctor told Brandon and Cash.

Willa felt as though someone had just taken her security blanket. Not good. Trusting Brandon was one thing but relying on him emotionally just wasn't very smart.

"I'm staying," Brandon insisted.

Cash said the same, and after staring at them, the doctor finally showed some emotion. She made a sound of mild annoyance and turned away from them.

Despite the little lecture Willa had just given herself about not leaning on Brandon, she was thankful that he would be nearby. After all, it was his name and his name only that she'd written on her hand.

"Should I lie down or something?" Willa asked.

Dr. Farris shook her head and started the DVD. "Just stay seated and focus on what you're seeing and hearing."

That sounded simple enough. Well, simple unless her short-term memory decided to take a hike. Since it'd been weeks since that had happened, Willa thought that part of this ordeal might be over, but she'd been wrong before.

The images started to appear on the screen. Someone was holding a video camera and recording their walk through the double automatic doors.

"We know from the exterior surveillance cameras that this is how you entered the building," the doctor explained. "Once you reach the fourth floor, your movements and what happens there are reenactments based on eyewitnesses." She kept her voice at a whisper and lowered the lights so that the only illumination came from the TV.

Willa forced herself to imagine that she was the one walking into the San Antonio Maternity Hospital. The greeting area didn't look familiar, but they quickly went through it and to the elevators. She pretended that it was her hand that pushed the button to take her to the fourth floor.

When *she* stepped into the elevator and the doors closed, Willa heard the music. There was nothing unusual about it, but it seemed familiar. The elevator seemed familiar, too. There were posters of mothers holding their newborns.

She felt her heart speed up a little when the doors swished open and she saw the fourth floor. Again, there was nothing unusual about it, and she guessed wrong about which direction she would take. The camera went to the left, past an empty waiting area. She saw the signs on the wall leading to the lab.

Why was she going there?

Because she was supposed to have some lab tests and then an ultrasound. That wasn't an actual memory, but she'd been told that by the police. Someone had called and told her she needed lab tests, but that had been a ruse to get her to the hospital.

The ruse had worked.

When the camera reached the lab desk, it stopped. Willa glanced around the corridor spread out in front of her and waited. She didn't have to wait long. She saw the ski-mask-wearing man racing toward her. He was armed.

"Don't close your eyes," the doctor insisted when Willa started to do just that.

It was a challenge, but she forced herself to watch as the man came closer and closer to the camera.

"Come with me," the man demanded, and he jammed the gun at her.

Willa didn't want to go with him. She wanted to run out of the hotel suite, far away from the camera and the nightmarish images, but she forced herself to stay put.

The gunman led her into the lab, past the cubicles where the techs drew blood. They went about twenty yards farther to a door with a sign that read: Authorized Personnel Only Beyond This Point. The man pressed in a code to get the door to open and led her into a room with computers and refrigerated storage containers.

They stopped moving, so Willa looked around as far

as the camera angle would allow. She took in as many details as she could manage. The glossy gray tile floor. The sterile white walls and ceiling. The way everything was arranged in precise order. The smell.

She froze.

The smell?

Did she really remember that?

Yes, she did. It wasn't the disinfectant odor like the rest of the hospital. This particular area smelled like some kind of lab chemical.

She felt the air-conditioning spill out from the overhead vents. The room was too cold, and she shivered. Willa waited for more sensations to come, and they did. They came at her hard and fast.

Willa gasped and pressed her fingers to her mouth. "Oh, God. I remember."

Chapter Eight

Brandon wasn't sure which of them looked more surprised, but he thought he might be the winner. When Dr. Farris had started that DVD, and Willa had started to watch, the last thing he expected was for Willa to remember anything.

But she apparently had.

She kept her gaze fastened to the screen where the hostage situation continued to play out. It seemed like such a simple exercise. Visual cues of a nightmare. But Willa kept repeating those two words as if it were a mantra. Or a warning.

I remember.

"What do you remember?" Dr. Farris asked, taking the words right out of Brandon's mouth.

Willa pressed her fingertips to both sides of her head and began to rock. Brandon went and sat beside her, then put his arm around her.

"It's okay." He tried to assure her, but he had no way of knowing if that was true.

"I remember the gunman taking me into the lab," Willa said. Her voice was barely a whisper, and he could feel her trembling.

Brandon tightened his grip, and her hands dropped to her lap. "What else?" he pressed.

Both the doctor and Cash moved closer, probably hoping they were all finally about to get answers. Brandon wanted those answers, too, but he hated that Willa was having to go through this all over again.

"The gunman took me into a secure area," she continued. "He pressed in some numbers on a key pad."

"Did he have the code written down?" Cash asked.

Willa nodded. "On a piece of paper he took from his pocket. He opened the door and pushed me inside. 'Go to the computer,' he told me. And I did. I went to the one where he pointed. It was on the far side of the room, sitting on a desk."

Cash leaned down so that he'd be eye level with Willa. "What did he want you to do?"

Before Willa could answer, Dr. Farris eased Cash out of the way. "No more questions, please. This will work best if Willa lets the memories come to her. And sometimes, these bits and pieces are all we'll get. To be honest with you, I wasn't sure it would even work this well."

Willa stared up at the doctor. "These aren't bits and pieces," she mumbled, her voice catching. "The gunman wanted me to hack into some secure files." She paused. "I did it because he put a gun to my head and said he would kill me and the baby if I didn't."

Brandon ignored the punch of anger he felt over what Willa had been through. He also ignored the doctor's no-question warning. "What files?"

"Ones that were being outsourced to the hospital,"

Willa readily answered. "The files belonged to the San Antonio Police Department, and they were biological samples that were to be used in several active cases. He wanted me to hack into the files and alter the data."

Definitely not bits and pieces. This was the sort of information that could blow this case wide open.

Brandon met Cash's stare. "Is it routine for SAPD to outsource tests to the hospital?"

Cash shook his head. "No. We usually use the Ranger lab in Austin, but there was a fire, and they got backlogged. I heard we were using some local hospitals to do some of the tests, but I didn't know it was this specific hospital."

"Dean Quinlan," Willa said out of the blue. "It was his name on the files. He was listed as the file manager. Do you know him?" she asked Cash.

"Yeah." Cash propped his hands on his hips and mumbled some profanity. "He's one of our CSIs. Well, he used to be anyway. He resigned shortly after the hostage incident to take a job elsewhere."

The doctor turned off the DVD and looked at Willa. "What else do you remember?"

Willa opened her mouth, hesitated, then closed it. "Nothing. That's all."

"You don't remember what specific files the gunman wanted you to hack into?" Cash demanded.

She shook her head. "No. I'm sorry. I remember sitting down at the computer, and I remember seeing Dean Quinlan's name as the file custodian, but that's it. Everything else after that is a blank." She started to tremble again, and Brandon pulled her closer to him.

Cash checked his watch. "I need to talk to Dean

Quinlan and anyone else who knew about those files being processed at the maternity hospital. I'll let you know what I find out." He took out his phone and headed into one of the suite's bedrooms.

"Your memory might continue to return," Dr. Farris told her. She paused to take Willa's pulse. "Sometimes, when you recall portions of the traumatic events, other details soon follow."

Willa nodded and pulled in a long breath. While that was good news for the investigation, Brandon knew this would be hell for Willa. After all, the gunman had likely been trying to kill her when she fell and injured her head.

"How are you feeling?" Dr. Farris asked.

"Exhausted." Willa adjusted her position and placed her head against Brandon's shoulder. "Could you give me a few minutes to gather my thoughts?"

Dr. Farris nodded, but she didn't look at all certain about leaving Willa. Finally, though, she walked toward the second bedroom, went inside and shut the door.

The moment the doctor was out of sight, Willa's head swooshed off his shoulder, and she stood. "I remembered some other things," she whispered.

Brandon froze. He didn't think her memory had returned just this instant. No. It had probably come with the other memories, but Willa had been smart not to tell all to the doctor. While Brandon still trusted Cash, he didn't know Dr. Farris and was glad Willa had withheld something that might put her in even more danger.

If that was possible.

"The gunman tried to call Dean Quinlan while we were in that secure area of the lab," Willa continued.

"He had Quinlan's name and number written on the back of the paper with the codes he used to get past the door."

"Did he actually speak to Quinlan?" Brandon, too, kept his voice at a whisper and stood so he could be closer to her.

She shook her head. "His cell phone couldn't get a signal in that part of the lab."

Probably because the walls had been reinforced for safety reasons, he thought. Labs and X-ray areas often have metal barriers to stop the harmful rays from getting into other parts of the building.

"The gunman was frustrated because he couldn't seem to read his notes," Willa explained. "He finally showed them to me, and that's when I saw the names of the files I was supposed to access. There were three of them—the first was Baby Martinez."

"That makes sense," Brandon concluded. "Misty Martinez was a San Antonio woman who was murdered, and her newborn was missing. Since Misty had stored the baby's umbilical cord at the maternity hospital, SAPD requested a DNA test so they could identify the biological father, who turned out to be her killer."

Willa's eyes widened. "Please tell me I didn't do anything to that DNA sample that allowed a killer to get away."

"No. The biological father, Gavin Cunningham, was arrested and got a life sentence."

She nodded but didn't relax. "The second name on the list was Jessie Beecham…" She paused, shook her head. "And Wes-somebody."

"Dunbar," Brandon provided. And he cursed.

Willa blinked. "You know these people?"

"I know *of* them. Jessie Beecham was a wealthy club owner with ties to the mob. He was murdered earlier this year, and the prime suspect was a rival club owner named Wes Dunbar."

SAPD had sent Brandon the initial reports of the investigation because Wes Dunbar had a country estate in Crockett Creek, Brandon's own town. At the time he'd read those reports, Brandon had no idea just how personal that case would become. Of course, the question was did the investigation into Jessie Beecham's murder have anything to do with Willa's situation?

Maybe not.

Maybe the culprit who'd hired Shore was simply someone who was tying up loose ends for the now-dead gunman who'd held her hostage. Maybe an unknown accomplice. What Brandon needed was more information, and that included a case update on Jessie Beecham's murder.

He glanced at the room where Cash had gone to make his call about the former CSI, Dean Quinlan. He looked at the room where the doctor was as well. And he got a really bad feeling about all of this. God knows who Dr. Farris had already told about Willa's regained memory, and Cash's calls and questions would almost certainly alert the wrong people.

"We need to get out of here?" Willa asked, obviously noticing the alarm on his face.

"Yeah." He grabbed her bag and her arm.

Brandon hoped to hell it wasn't too late.

WILLA WAS BEYOND TIRED of being on the run, but she knew Brandon was right to get them out of there.

Maybe both Cash and Dr. Farris were on the up-and-up, but that didn't mean someone, including Martin Shore, would get word that she had remembered what had gone on in the lab the day the maternity hostages were taken.

Brandon eased the suite door shut behind them and got them moving to the elevator. He had her bag slung over his shoulder and kept one hand on her and the other within easy reach of his gun. Willa held her breath until they were in the elevator and the doors slid shut. They weren't out of danger yet, not by a long shot, but she wanted to put as much distance as possible between the suite and them.

"What do we do now?" she asked and mentally cursed the fatigue and fog in her head.

She should have already figured that out for herself, but here she was again relying on Brandon. Once they were safely away from the hotel, she had to find some time to come up with a new plan—and a couple of backup ones.

"We need a vehicle and some cash," Brandon answered. "I have to get you to a safe place, and we can't get there on foot with Shore this close and every cop in San Antonio looking for us."

That "safe place" part certainly sounded good to her, but was it even doable?

"I have some cash in the bag," Willa let him know. "About five hundred dollars."

But she would need a lot more than that if she had to go into hiding for any length of time. Which she probably would. That meant making a trip to the banks in Austin or San Antonio, so she could get to one of her safety deposit boxes where she'd stashed more money.

Brandon stopped the elevator on the second floor. "It's too risky to go into the main part of the lobby," he told her.

So, they left the elevator and went into the stairwell. Brandon stopped long enough to look at the emergency exit route map that was on the wall. Willa looked as well and wasn't pleased that the stairs ended so close to the lobby. They would still be in sight of the front desk and entrance. But hopefully not for long. There appeared to be a back exit just off a coffee shop. She prayed the door there wasn't rigged with an alarm.

When they reached the bottom of the stairs, Brandon stopped and peered out through the glass insert in the door. "No sign of Shore or other cops," he relayed to her.

That didn't give her any sense of relief. Shore had gotten the jump on them before, and it could happen again.

They left the meager cover of the stairwell and stepped out into the back part of the lobby, which was just ten or fifteen feet from the coffee shop. They only made it a few steps before Brandon pulled her into a shallow recessed area that led to the ladies' room. He maneuvered her behind him.

"Shhh," he warned.

Her heart went to her knees, and she came up on her tiptoes so she could look over his shoulder. Willa dreaded what she would see.

There were several people milling around in the lobby and two hotel employees behind the check-in desk. She certainly didn't see the apparent threat Brandon thought was there, but she had no intention of leaving their hiding place, either. She stood there waiting with her breath held.

Two of the people in the lobby picked up their suitcases and headed for the front exit.

That's when Willa spotted the man.

He was on the other side of the check-in desk, partly hidden behind a massive plant.

Oh, God.

It was Martin Shore.

He was volleying glances between the elevator and the front door. And she recognized what he held in his hand.

Her PDA.

Willa clamped her teeth over her bottom lip so that her gasp wouldn't be loud enough to draw anyone's attention—especially Shore's. How had he actually found them? Had Cash or Dr. Farris alerted him, or had Shore merely followed her PDA and guessed their location? His presence could be a fishing expedition, but it didn't matter. He was there—so close—and that meant the danger was there again too.

The baby began to kick, hard, and since her belly was pressed against Brandon's back, he no doubt felt it. He glanced over his shoulder at her but then nailed his attention back on Shore.

They couldn't wait long in the alcove without someone noticing them, and it wouldn't be wise to try to hide out in the ladies' room where they would be trapped. Soon, if not already, Cash and the doctor would realize they were missing and would come looking for them.

That would no doubt confirm to Shore that they were still in the building. Besides, she didn't want anyone, including Cash and Dr. Farris, to find them. Willa only wanted to get out of there.

"We need to move fast when we get outside," Brandon whispered.

Willa nodded and hoped that *fast* would be fast enough.

Part of her wondered if it was best just to have a showdown with Shore. Here and now. After all, Brandon was a cop. He knew how to take down a killer. But Shore wasn't an ordinary killer. He wouldn't give up without a hard fight, and that would mean bullets flying. Innocent people could be killed. And once again, her precious baby would be in harm's way.

"Now!" Brandon ordered.

He turned, not abruptly though. He kept his movement unhurried. He also kept her in front of him so that he was between Shore and her. Brandon was protecting her yet again.

The dozen or so steps to the exit seemed to take a lifetime, but Willa knew it was only a few seconds. Brandon shoved open the door and got her outside.

The burst of cold air hit her in the face, but she didn't take the time to catch her breath. Brandon got them moving, not across the parking lot where they could easily be seen. He led her toward the back of the hotel, and they hurried past the service and delivery entrances. There were men unloading boxes, but none seemed to pay any attention to them.

Brandon kept watch behind them and then stopped when they reached the corner of the building. There was about ten yards of wide-open space between the hotel and the next building, which was a one-story chain restaurant.

"Let's move," Brandon insisted, and they quickly got across to the back of the restaurant.

They repeated that process for three more buildings, putting some distance between the hotel and them.

Willa heard the sirens, but it only heightened her fear. However, Brandon paused and looked out as if he were considering the possibility of going to the responding officers.

"Please tell me you're not going out there," she whispered.

"Not a chance." He grabbed her arm again and got them moving farther away from the hotel and from those approaching sirens.

"Then where are we going once we get a car?" Willa demanded.

Brandon lifted her hand so she would have a reminder of what she'd written there. "You have to trust me a little longer, Willa. Because I'm taking you to the one place I know where I can keep you safe."

Chapter Nine

They were *home*.

Well, they were at *his* home anyway, Willa amended.

It was apparently the one place he knew where he could keep her safe. Maybe he felt that way because of the two dogs. The minute they turned into the gravel driveway that led to the isolated house, two Dobermans came racing toward them. Neither dog looked very welcoming, and they barked and chased the car.

It wasn't exactly a friendly greeting.

The trek to his rural Crockett Creek house hadn't been a friendly one, either. It'd taken them more than an hour to get far enough away from the hotel and to a pay phone he thought might be safe to use. He'd called one of his deputies, Pete Sanchez, a fiftysomething-year-old man who had arrived to pick them up in San Antonio, so he could then drive them out to Brandon's place.

The drive had been long and tedious. Along with bathroom stops to accommodate Willa and the round-about route the deputy had used to get them to the small Texas town, the trip was more than three hours. Willa was beyond exhausted, and that was probably a good thing because the exhaustion numbed some of the fear.

Temporarily, anyway.

The fear returned when she studied the house itself. Despite the barking dogs, it wasn't a fortress, that's for sure. It looked more like, well, a home.

Deputy Sanchez pulled to a stop in front of the porch and steps.

"Are you sure we'll be safe here?" Willa asked, eyeing the cottage-style house.

With the iron-gray sky and the icy drizzle spitting at them, the house was the only spot of color in the winter landscape. It was a cheery shade of yellow and had dark green shutters and door. There were even flower boxes anchored beneath the windows. It wasn't what she expected from a dark and brooding small-town Texas sheriff.

"The place was painted like this when I bought it," Brandon mumbled, probably sensing her surprise. "Wait here," he told her.

Brandon drew his gun, and just like that, the fatigue could no longer numb the fear. Willa sat there on the backseat of the deputy's four-door black Ford and watched as Brandon got out. He didn't say anything to the dogs. He merely lifted his left hand, and they both went silent. The pair followed Brandon up the steps and to the door he then unlocked. However, they didn't go inside. The dogs waited for him on the porch.

"Please, don't let there be anyone in there," Willa mumbled. But she obviously didn't mumble it softly enough because the deputy eased around in the seat and looked at her.

"Butch and Sundance wouldn't have let anyone inside," Deputy Sanchez drawled. "Brandon's just being extra cautious. If the dogs are alive and kickin', then no one got near the place and remained in one piece."

Even though Willa didn't like the idea of being around attack dogs, it was better than having no outside protection against a professional assassin.

Pete kept the windshield wipers on, and they scraped away at the sleety drizzle, smearing the ice on the glass.

"I'm assuming Brandon doesn't need the dogs for security," she commented. "Because I'd figured Crockett Creek was a safe town."

"Don't worry, it is. I think the dogs help Brandon make sure his privacy stays private. It's probably why he lives all the way out here by himself. This place is a good ten miles outside of town."

That said a lot about the man whose baby she was carrying. A private man. A man she trusted, she reminded herself.

A man she wanted.

Willa quickly tried to push that thought aside, but it flashed right back in her head. She huffed. Her memory was still a mess in parts, and yet she could remember in complete, agonizing detail every twinge of attraction she felt for a man who placed a high value on privacy and keeping secrets.

"So, who takes care of the place and the dogs when he's out of town?" Willa wanted to know. It hadn't occurred to her until now that Brandon might have a girlfriend.

"His neighbor's boy does that for him."

"Neighbor?" she questioned. Not a girlfriend. Though she didn't see a nearby house or any other signs of a neighbor.

"Zach Grange," the deputy provided. "He raised the dogs from pups, and he's about the only one other than Brandon that they trust to get near them. I figure Brandon likes having 'em around. He worked canines for a while in Special Forces, you know."

No, she didn't know. That was another of the secrets he hadn't been ready to volunteer.

Brandon came back out and returned to the car so he could open her door and take her overnight bag. The wet, cold air came right at her, sending a chill straight through her clothes. Brandon thanked his deputy, and the man tipped his Stetson and drove away.

"Will the dogs bite?" she asked, eyeing them as they went up the steps. Even though it was freezing, literally, she didn't hurry because she didn't want to alarm them.

"They won't bite you." And he aimed a glance at both, one that was effective because the two remained docile on the porch as Willa went past them and into the house.

Her first impression was that the place was toasty warm. Thank goodness. And everything was neat and orderly. There were no clothes lying around, no clutter. The living room had been painted a soft cream color that complemented the slate-blue sofa and recliner. He had a flat-screen TV mounted on the wall above the fireplace.

Other than the winter weather outside, there were no signs of Christmas here. Like her place in Austin.

Hard to concentrate on the holidays when their lives were on the line.

"The kitchen's through here," he explained, pointing through a doorway.

Willa looked inside. Neat and orderly there, too.

"The bathroom's over there." He pointed to the first room off the hall that fed off the living room.

"Is it okay if I take a shower?" she asked.

"Of course." He handed Willa her overnight bag and walked into the kitchen. "Then I'll fix us something to eat, and you can get some rest."

All three of those—a shower, food and rest— sounded heavenly, and Willa headed to the bathroom. But then, she stopped.

"I want the truth," she told him, turning back around to face him. "Will Shore come here looking for us?"

Brandon had been about to open the fridge, but his hand paused in midair. He looked at her and then crossed the room toward her.

"He might," Brandon confessed. "The dogs won't let him get close, but he could try to neutralize them."

Neutralize. What a benign word for *kill.*

"I have a security system wired to all the windows and doors," Brandon continued. "It came with the house, and even though I've never had an occasion to use it, I will now that you're here."

"Good." And she heard herself repeat it several times. Because she suddenly felt shaky, Willa placed the bag on the floor and held the doorframe to steady herself.

Brandon caught onto her. "Are you okay?"

She managed a nod. "I'm not very good with this whole trying-to-kill-us thing."

"Few people are good at that," he mumbled. He pulled her into his arms. "And you don't want to be around them if they are."

Since that sounded, well, personal, she eased back and met him eye to eye. She'd done that so she could see his expression when she asked him what he meant by that. But the question faded from her mind when she stared at him.

Mercy.

There it was again. That damn attraction. An itch, some people called it. Willa just thought of it as an itchy nuisance. It was clouding her judgment and drawing her to a man she should be questioning. Instead, she was falling for him.

"What?" he asked.

She had no intention of telling him what she was thinking. A man like Brandon would likely turn and run—after he made sure she was safe, that is. He was a natural protector. An alpha male. And she instinctively knew that a pregnant woman falling hard for him would take him right out of his very narrow comfort zone.

Willa shook her head to try to blow off his question, but she found herself leaning in closer to him. Why, why, why couldn't she just back away?

Because she didn't want to.

Because she wanted Brandon.

He reached to brush a strand of hair off her face, but he didn't pull back his hand. His fingers stayed, touching her cheek.

"You've been through a lot," he said as if that explained the coil of heat that was simmering inside her.

She made a sound of agreement and leaned in. Willa only intended to touch her mouth to his. Just a taste of what her body was begging her to have. But Brandon made a sound of his own.

Not of agreement.

The husky sound rumbled in his throat, and his hand went from her cheek to the back of her neck. He snapped her to him.

And it wasn't just a touch.

BRANDON FORGOT ALL ABOUT the danger. About the fatigue. About all the other things he should be doing. However, he didn't forget about this need inside him. A need that only Willa seemed capable of satisfying.

Why the hell did he want her like this?

He didn't have an answer for that, and it didn't seem to matter to his mouth, or to the rest of his body. He just hauled her as close to him as she could possibly get, and he kissed her as if he had a right to do exactly that.

He didn't have that right, though.

Kisses and caresses would just lead her on. But that still didn't stop him.

He tightened the grip he had on the back of her neck and angled her head so he could deepen the kiss. She tasted like…Willa. It was a taste he'd already sampled, and while there was the whole forbidden-fruit thing going on here, his response seemed about much more than that. He'd had forbidden fruit before, and it'd never tasted this good.

She made that mind-blowing sound of pleasure deep within her throat and pressed as hard against him as he did against her. They pulled away, only to catch their breath and, as if starved for each other, went right back for another round.

Soon, though, the kiss and the body-to-body contact wasn't enough. Soon, certain parts of him started to demand more. That was Brandon's cue to pull away, and he tried. But Willa held on, and he didn't put up much of a fight.

"I'm on fire," she mumbled against his mouth.

That was something he didn't need to hear, but it wasn't something he could forget, either. It was a primal invitation to his overly aroused body, and his instincts were to scoop her up in his arms and haul her off to bed.

That couldn't happen, of course.

Brandon repeated that to himself but still didn't pull away. Instead, he dropped some kisses on her neck and cupped her left breast with his hand.

"Still on fire," she let him know, and she added more of those sounds of silky feminine pleasure.

Willa went after his neck as well and landed a few kisses in one of his very sensitive spots. Too sensitive. More of that, and a trip to the bed would happen whether it should or not.

Brandon forced himself to pull back.

Willa's breath was gusting now, and his wasn't much slower. They stared at each other, too close for him not to consider just jumping right back in. But he didn't. If a simple kiss was leading her on, then this was a dozen steps past that at a time when Willa was most vulnerable. She was pregnant and scared. And he was taking advantage of that and this attraction between them.

She ran her tongue over her bottom lip and made another sound of pleasure. Brandon's body clenched, and he took a huge step back.

"So?" she said. "What happens now?"

No way was he going to answer that. Because a response—any response—could get him in even hotter water.

"Ah," she mumbled when he glanced away. "I guess that means we aren't going to do *that*."

"No," he agreed. "Wrong time, wrong place. Hell… wrong everything." Brandon mumbled some harsher profanity under his breath.

"Wrong man?" she concluded.

"Especially that." He glanced away again and was sorry he'd said anything.

"You have that look again, as if I just poked a stick at a raw wound. You obviously have secrets you don't want to share."

She grabbed his chin and drew his gaze back to hers. "Since you've saved my life more than once in the past twenty-four hours, I would tell you my deepest darkest secret…if I could remember it."

She smiled.

He didn't.

"You don't remember your secrets?" he asked. This was the first time it had occurred to him that she hadn't regained her full memory after watching that DVD in the hotel suite.

Willa shrugged. "I'd like to say yes to that, but there are still blanks." She drew in a quick breath. "On the drive over, I kept trying to piece things together, but I don't remember how I ended up on the floor of that hospital."

Good. Maybe she wouldn't regain those horrific memories. She had remembered what files the gunman had forced her to access, and that had to be enough. Willa had already had enough stress without recalling an attack that had left her in a coma.

She touched his face again, turning him in her direction. "I sense you're pushing me away. That's probably for the best, if I were in a sane mode right now. I'm not. I'm in pregnancy mode where I need to protect this baby at all costs. I figure you're my best bet for that protection because you have a genetic link."

He stared at her. "Yeah," he settled for saying.

Brandon almost left it at that. Almost. But for some reason he decided that Willa deserved something better. A better explanation. And she certainly deserved something better than him.

"My birth father is a man named Wade Decalley," Brandon heard himself say. "My mother never talked about him much, and a few years ago, I found out why." He paused long enough to gather his breath. "He's a convicted serial killer, and he's spent the last thirteen years on death row."

Brandon realized it was the first time he'd said that out loud. The first time he'd actually told anyone the truth about his father.

Willa didn't blink. Didn't gasp. She merely put her fingers on his arm and rubbed gently. "I'm sorry."

"No need," he practically snapped. "I didn't know about him when I agreed to donate the semen I'd stored for my military tour in the Middle East."

Now she blinked, and she gave him an ah-ha kind of look. "Now, I get it. You don't want to pass on your DNA to a child because of your father."

"But I did anyway. I'm sorry for that, Willa. I'm sorry you didn't get the biological father you thought you were getting for this baby."

The corner of her mouth lifted, but she was also blinking back tears. "I think this baby girl has an amazing biological dad, one who would risk his own life to protect her." Willa leaned in and kissed his cheek. "I don't regret her having your DNA."

"You might," he mumbled.

She huffed, pulled away from him and fluttered her fingers in the direction of the bathroom. "I think I'll grab that shower now."

Brandon hoped it would help her relax, especially after their kissing session and his confession about his family *legacy*. He sure as hell could use something to help him relax, too, but he had too much to do. While he fixed Willa something to eat, he needed to call and try to get some information about Jessie Beecham's murder and the files that the gunman had wanted Willa to tamper with.

That meant contacting Cash.

Brandon took a prepaid cell phone from the kitchen drawer. A phone that couldn't be traced. He'd bought it on impulse, a throwback to his Special Ops days when he had been trained to be prepared for anything. At the time of the purchase, he had figured it would never be used, that he would spend the rest of his life as a sheriff, not doing anything that required a prepaid cell. But he needed to return to his roots in covert ops in order to keep Willa safe.

However, it would have to end there.

Once he had the answers they needed and Martin Shore and the danger had been neutralized, there would be only one thing left for him to do.

The best thing he could do for both Willa and the baby was to get as far away from them as possible.

Chapter Ten

Willa sat at the cozy kitchen table and ate the turkey and cheese sandwich Brandon had fixed for her. She wasn't actually hungry, but she forced herself to eat because of the baby.

Brandon's own sandwich lay untouched on the table across from her, and instead of eating, he was pacing while he talked on a cell phone. Since he'd been on the phone when she came out of the shower, she had no idea how long this conversation had been going on. But she did know that he was talking to Cash.

And Brandon obviously wasn't happy about the answers he was hearing.

"Now you think Dr. Farris could be responsible for the leak?" Brandon challenged. He didn't wait for an answer. He went to the laptop sitting on a corner desk and pressed some keys. "Because before we even met the doctor, Martin Shore found us at the safe house that SAPD provided."

He paused, and she could hear the faint sound of Cash's voice on the other end of the line. Unfortunately, she couldn't hear what he was saying.

"You do that," he told Cash. "You dig into Dr. Farris's

background, and I'll do the same. If the woman is dirty, I want her arrested."

So did Willa. She cringed because she'd actually been in the room with the person who might want her dead. And she'd trusted the doctor. Well, she'd trusted her enough to watch that DVD that had spurred her memory and almost certainly created more danger.

"Cash thinks the doctor is the leak?" Willa mouthed.

He shook his head and held his hand over the speaker end of the cell. "I think he's grasping at straws. He has no proof."

And they didn't have proof of Cash's innocence, either.

"Good," Brandon said several moments later, removing his hand so he could continue his call to Cash. The printer next to the laptop began to spit out something. "Because I'd like to talk with Dean Quinlan, too. Yes, you can do that. Have him call me at this number."

Dean Quinlan—the former CSI whose name had been on the files at the hospital. Willa didn't think she'd actually met the man, but like Brandon, she wanted to ask him questions about his involvement in all this.

"No, I'm not bringing Willa in," Brandon insisted. "And no, I'm not telling you where we are." He hung up. "Don't worry. Cash didn't send the fax. My deputy did, so Cash doesn't know we're here." He snatched the piece of paper from the printer.

"Recognize him?" Brandon asked, sliding the paper across the table toward her. It was a picture of a brown-haired man with a thin face.

Willa shook her head. "No. Who is he?"

"That's Dean Quinlan."

She took a harder look at the man who seemed to be at the center of everything. Was he the person who'd hired Shore to kill her? He didn't look like a killer, but Dean Quinlan could want her dead because she might be able to prove his involvement in the maternity hostage situation.

"He wants to talk to you?" she asked.

"Yeah. But don't expect Quinlan to confess to anything. Cash questioned him over the phone—Quinlan refused to meet with him—but the man claims he's innocent."

And he might be. But someone was guilty. "What about the actual lab samples at the maternity hospital? Did I tamper with them?" She shook her head, huffed. "Because I only remember hacking into them."

"Cash claims the test results were fine. They did a duplicate set of tests at another site and came up with the same results." He sat down across from her and met her gaze. "Of course, if you managed to tamper with the actual samples, then the duplicate test would give the same results."

Willa put her sandwich back on the plate and tried to recall any other details. But her mind just wouldn't let her go there.

"If I somehow contaminated or corrupted the samples, then how would I prove that?" she wanted to know.

"You can't. But it's possible they could exhume Jessie Beecham's body to get what they need. There were two

DNA samples in the files you accessed," Brandon explained. "They were taken from tissue found beneath Beecham's fingernails."

"Jessie Beecham," she repeated. "The club owner with ties to the mob who was found murdered."

Another nod. "But this wasn't a mob hit. Too messy for that. It appears Beecham had been in some kind of physical altercation with his killer before he was struck on the head with a blunt object. His wallet, gun and phone were all missing, so SAPD suspected the motive might be robbery."

Willa gave that some thought. "Or maybe it was meant to look like a robbery?"

"Yeah." And he paused again. "So, SAPD wanted a fast turnaround on the DNA they collected from his fingernails because they wanted a quick arrest. Beecham's allies were making a lot of noise and blaming Beecham's rival. SAPD thought they might have a mob war on their hands. Since the lab in Austin was out of commission thanks to the fire, they sent it to the secure area of the San Antonio Maternity Hospital."

Which had turned out not to be so secure thanks to the gunman, and her. "Who would have known the samples were there?" she immediately asked.

"Anyone in SAPD." Brandon mumbled some frustrated profanity. "Or someone who worked in the hospital lab itself."

In other words, there were too many people involved to narrow it down to one specific suspect. She already didn't trust Dr. Farris, Cash and this Dean Quinlan, but she would possibly have to add many more to her list.

Brandon took the photo from her and stared at it. "According to Cash, the DNA samples were held in a secure vault, and the handful of hospital staff who had access to that area all had the proper security clearances. They've all checked out and are no longer suspects."

"Well, someone gave the gunman the code to get into the vault area because it was written on the paper he took from his pocket."

"Cash believes the gunman could have gotten the info after the hostage situation started. A lab tech was killed within minutes after the gunmen stormed the hospital. It's possible the gunman threatened to kill the tech, and he coughed up the code."

"And the gunman killed him anyway," Willa supplied. Then she thought of something else. "The gunman tried to call Dean Quinlan."

"Quinlan denies that," Brandon grumbled. "But I don't buy it. Quinlan could have been bought off."

"By whom?"

"By Wes Dunbar, the rival club owner. Jessie Beecham and he were long-time enemies. They could have gotten into an altercation that resulted in Beecham's death." He dropped the picture onto the table. "But the DNA samples didn't prove that. The DNA belonged to a homeless man with a criminal record a mile long."

"So, this homeless man was arrested?" Willa asked.

"He was. And his court-appointed lawyer did a plea bargain. The guy's already in jail for manslaughter."

But he could be innocent. All of this, including the hostage situation itself, could have been orchestrated to put the blame for murder on a homeless man when the real killer was still out there.

It didn't take Willa long to come up with a possible identity for the real killer. "Wes Dunbar, the rival club owner, could have murdered Beecham and then paid off the CSI, Dean Quinlan, to tamper with the evidence."

Brandon nodded and pulled in a hard breath.

So, why was there the threat of another hostage situation? Had someone else decided to do the same thing as Wes Dunbar? If so, Willa's memory wasn't going to be of any help. That caused her to groan. As long as the danger was there, she was anchored to Brandon. Part of her—okay, her body—was all right with that. She wanted to sleep with him, and she was certain that was driving a lot of her other desires.

But it was clear that Brandon wasn't in this for a one-night stand or a happily ever after. She didn't need her memory to feel that he wanted to be out of her life. And that meant solving this case. The sooner that was done, the sooner they could both go back to the way things were before. That's what she wanted.

Willa repeated that.

It still didn't ring true.

She forced herself to focus just on the case. "Any suggestions as to what I should do next?"

Brandon's jaw muscles stirred, but before he could answer, his phone rang. Even though the cell didn't have caller ID, she figured it was Cash. Hopefully, the cop would have information that would help them.

Brandon didn't say a word when he took the call. He merely put the phone to his ear. A moment later, she saw the surprise, and then the concern, go through his eyes.

"Dean Quinlan," he said.

Though the sound of the man's name caused her heart to race, this was good news. Well, potentially good. Dean was the next step in getting information because even if he was simply trying to cover his guilt, he could still slip up and tell them if Wes Dunbar or someone else hired him to have those DNA samples tampered with.

"A meeting?" Brandon questioned.

Willa waited with her breath held. She didn't relish the idea of seeing this man, but again, it might be the beginning of the end to the danger.

"All right," Brandon said a moment later. "I'll meet you at my office in Crockett Creek." He paused again. "No, I can't be there that soon. I'm at least two hours out."

That was a lie, of course, to try to conceal their real location.

Brandon checked his watch. "I'll meet you there at three o'clock. And Quinlan, my suggestion is you'd better have answers. The *right answers*. Or I'll find a reason to arrest you."

It seemed as if Brandon was about to hang up, but he stopped. "What do you mean?" he demanded from Dean. "Who's trying to kill you?"

Whatever Dean said, it caused Brandon's jaw muscles to go to work again. He cursed when he slapped the phone shut.

"Someone's trying to kill Dean Quinlan?" Willa asked.

"Yeah." And that's all Brandon said for several moments. "He claims Cash wants him dead. And Quinlan says he has something to prove it."

Chapter Eleven

Deputy Pete Sanchez parked in front of the back entrance to the Crockett Creek sheriff's office. It was Brandon's usual parking space, but before today, he'd never felt like checking his too-familiar surroundings before he exited. Of course, that had plenty to do with Willa being with him.

Brandon tried to give her a reassuring glance before he got her out of the vehicle and hurried her inside. He'd already apologized a couple of times for having to bring her for what would likely be a high-stress meeting with Dean Quinlan. However, the alternative was leaving her alone at his place, and that wasn't going to happen. Brandon had no intention of letting her out of his sight.

Martin Shore was still out there somewhere. And even though it was Christmas Eve, the holiday season wouldn't stop the hired gun from striking again.

Brandon heard the voices the moment he stepped inside. He was already on full alert, but those voices upped his anxiety. One of the voices belonged to his other deputy, Sheila Gafford, a thirty-year law-enforcement veteran who didn't normally raise her voice. But that's exactly what she was doing now.

"I told you to sit down and wait," Sheila ordered.

"And I told you that I will see the sheriff *now,*" the man responded.

Brandon didn't recognize the voice, but he sure as heck recognized anger when he heard it. This guy was outraged about something.

"Wait here with Willa," Brandon told Pete, and he left them in his office while he went to the front of the building. Sheila was there, staring down a tall man wearing a business suit.

The man looked past the deputy and glared when he spotted Brandon making his way toward them.

"A problem?" Brandon asked Sheila.

His deputy rolled her coffee-brown eyes and huffed. "This is Mr. Wes—"

"Dunbar," the visitor interrupted.

Well, Brandon hadn't had to go looking for the devil after all because here was his number one suspect, just a few feet away.

"Are you Sheriff Ruiz?" Wes demanded.

Even though he was rail thin, he had a booming voice, and everything about him screamed money. The suit was high-priced. Haircut, too. And judging from his perfect nails, the man had regular manicures. He didn't look the sort to do his own dirty work, but then Jessie Beecham had likely been killed in the heat of an argument.

"I'm Sheriff Ruiz," Brandon confirmed. "What do you want?"

"To talk to you. I heard about that former maternity

hostage, Willa Marks. She's connected to what happened in the hospital that day."

"Yeah? What makes you think that?" Brandon didn't intend to volunteer anything.

"Don't play stupid with me. Protect her all you want. She's not the reason I'm here. But I figure that sewer rat, Dean Quinlan, is dying to get to her, and since I'm dying to get to Quinlan, I figured the fastest way to do that would be through you."

Brandon glanced around to see if Dean was already there. He wasn't. Though he should have been. He was nearly a half hour late. Of course, maybe Wes Dunbar's impromptu visit had something to do with that. However, Brandon spotted an expensive black luxury sedan he didn't recognize. It no doubt belonged to Wes, and the man behind the wheel was probably his driver.

"Why do you want to get to Dean Quinlan?" Brandon asked.

"Simple. He's trying to pin Jessie Beecham's murder on me by claiming I'm the one who hired those idiots to take the maternity hostages."

"Dean told you this?"

"Didn't have to. I hear things, and I don't like what I'm hearing. Jessie's killer is already behind bars, and Jessie's in hell. Case closed."

Maybe closed but not necessarily resolved. "Did you try to kill Willa Marks?" Brandon didn't expect a straight answer, but he figured it wouldn't hurt to ask.

"I have no reason to kill her. As far as I can tell she's not blabbing to the cops that I'm Jessie's killer. Plus, I heard her head's all messed up. She doesn't remember her own name, much less what happened at the hospital that day."

Brandon wanted to punch that smug look off Wes's face. But while that might give him some temporary satisfaction, it wouldn't help Willa.

"You seem to know a lot about Ms. Marks," Brandon commented. It was a fishing expedition. He wanted to know if Wes was getting his info from anyone in SAPD.

But Wes didn't bite. A dry smile bent his mouth for several short seconds, and he aimed his finger at Brandon. "If Dean Quinlan gets in touch with you, my advice is not to believe a word he says."

"Why would he lie to me?"

"To cover his scrawny butt. I figure he screwed up something. He was a CSI after all. He screwed up something, and then tried to put the blame on anyone but himself." His finger landed against his own chest. "Well, that blame better not come anywhere near me. Got that?"

Wes didn't wait for Brandon's response. He turned and stormed out. Wes climbed into a sleek black limo waiting for him just outside and the driver took off.

"Never known a Christmas Eve like this one," Sheila grumbled. She pushed her dark, gray-threaded hair away from her face. "I swear, the phone's been ringing off the hook. Four messages in the past two hours—all from Dr. Lenora Farris."

Brandon cursed. "What does she want?"

"Same thing as the bozo who just left. She wants to talk to you. Says it's important. Says you're to return her calls ASAP." She lifted her hands in the air. "Don't these people have anything better to do over the holidays than pester us?"

Apparently not. "Did Dean Quinlan show up?"

"Not yet." She checked the clock on the wall. "Guess you want me to wait here until he does?"

"I do. Thanks, Sheila. But keep the door locked. I don't want just anyone waltzing in here unannounced."

The woman complained under her breath, as Brandon had known she would. She obviously didn't like being called into work on her off day, but she would stay. And she would do everything within her power to help him protect Willa. That was all he could ask for at the moment. But once this meeting with Dean was over, Brandon had to figure out his next move. It probably wasn't wise to stay around Crockett Creek now that both Wes and Dean knew he was there.

He walked back to his office where Pete was standing guard in the doorway. Willa was there, too, peeking out, and judging from her expression, she'd heard everything Wes had said.

"He's gone?" she asked.

Brandon nodded and tipped his head to Pete to get him moving as well. Pete went in the direction of the deputies' office on the other side of the reception desk.

Since Willa looked ready to collapse, Brandon pulled her into his arms. "Wes was just blowing smoke," he assured her. But the fact that he felt the need to blow smoke said a lot.

Wes was acting like a guilty man.

Of course, he had the strongest motive of all their suspects. If that had been his DNA underneath Jessie

Beecham's fingernails, then Wes could have been convicted of murder. Now, the question was had he killed Beecham and then orchestrated the hostage situation to cover it up?

If so, then Wes would almost certainly want Willa dead.

Brandon was about to offer Willa more reassurances, but movement stopped him. It hadn't come from the hall but from Willa's middle.

The baby was kicking.

He pulled back slightly and looked down.

"Soccer practice," Willa joked.

There was certainly a lot of movement, much more than he'd expected for an unborn child. And some of the kicks were hard, too. He could actually see the thumps against Willa's top.

Without thinking, Brandon slid his palm over her belly. And he froze. He shouldn't be doing this. This was something a real father should do, and it was far too intimate. More intimate than the hot kissing session they'd shared in his kitchen.

"Amazing, isn't it?" Willa asked.

Brandon made a sound that could have meant anything, and he jerked back his hand. "It must hurt."

"No," she insisted. She stared at him. "It's okay, Brandon. A touch doesn't commit you to anything. Kisses don't, either."

"But sex would," he mumbled before he could stop himself. Hell. What was wrong with him? First he couldn't control his hand, and now he couldn't control his mouth.

"Depends on the sex."

His gaze fired to hers, and he expected to see another of those teasing half smiles. But no smile. She looked dead serious. Then, she huffed.

"Sorry," she whispered. "I guess there's no such thing as no-strings-attached sex when it comes to us."

"No," he agreed.

He wanted to explain that he wasn't the father his baby deserved, but Willa had already heard it. It obviously hadn't sunk in because he still saw the welcoming look in her eyes. For a woman who distrusted nearly everyone, it was a powerful, and touching, burden to place on him.

Brandon heard someone knock. The sound came from the back where Willa and he had entered. He drew his gun, motioned for her to stay put and went to look out the sliver of a reinforced side window.

Thankfully, the man looked exactly like his photograph so Brandon had no trouble recognizing their visitor.

It was Dean Quinlan.

Dean's gaze was slashing all around the parking lot as if he expected someone to jump out and attack. Which might be close to the truth. Brandon didn't see any sign of a weapon, so he opened the door.

"What was Wes Dunbar doing here?" Dean demanded.

Brandon didn't even try to relieve the man's nerves. "Looking for you, I think."

Dean tried to bolt inside, but Brandon stopped and frisked him. He wasn't carrying concealed, but he did have an envelope gripped in his left hand.

Brandon stepped aside so the man could enter, but he

kept himself between Dean and his office where he'd left Willa. Even though he was a good six inches shorter than Brandon, Dean tried to look over his shoulder.

"Did you tell Wes that I was coming here?" Dean asked. He continued to glance around, and there were beads of sweat on his forehead despite the chilly winter temperature outside.

"No. Did you?"

Dean looked at him as if he'd lost his mind. "Why would I tell a scumbag like him where I was? He could be the one who wants me dead." He paused. "Well, maybe it's him."

"You got more than one person trying to kill you?" Brandon asked.

"Maybe," Dean repeated and shook his head. "Look, someone's been trying to kill me, and I think it might be the same person who's after Willa Marks. There was a story in the newspaper about someone blowing up her house."

Brandon tried not to curse but failed. He was all for freedom of the press, but the less printed about Willa, the safer she might be.

"Who's trying to kill us?" Brandon heard someone ask. He groaned because it was Willa's voice and he heard her making her way toward them. He shot her a look, warning to go back to his office.

She ignored him and kept her attention pinned to Dean.

Dean studied her a moment and then handed Brandon the envelope. Brandon didn't put away his weapon, and he handed the envelope to Willa so she could open it.

There was a single black-and-white picture inside.

It was a grainy photo taken in what appeared to be a parking lot, and it took Brandon a moment to figure out that he was looking at a picture of three people.

Wes Dunbar, Dr. Lenora Farris.

And Cash.

Ironically, it was the face of his old friend that was the clearest.

"I've been keeping an eye on Cash and Wes," Dean explained. "I thought one or both of them might be trying to set me up to take the fall for that hostage situation."

"Why would they do that?" Brandon wanted to know.

"Because I think Wes did kill Jessie Beecham, and I think that DNA sample in the lab would have proven it."

Brandon couldn't argue with that. "But why would Cash want to frame you?" He handed the picture to Willa so she could see it as well.

Dean gave Brandon another are-you-out-of-your-mind look. "I've checked on you, and I know you and Cash are old friends. But Cash isn't the man you knew way back when. He's friends with Wes now—did he tell you that?"

No. Cash hadn't. And Brandon wasn't sure he believed Dean. Still, there was the photo.

"That picture proves nothing," Willa said, probably sensing Brandon's conflicting emotions.

"It proves the three of them were together," Dean countered. "And I think they were together for one reason—to figure out how they could cover up the fact that Wes killed his old rival."

Brandon could see one huge flaw in that theory. "Then why involve Dr. Farris? If Wes wanted someone to cover up his crime, he would go to Cash or some other dirty cop."

"You don't know?" But it wasn't really a question, and Dean seemed more than eager to dole out this tidbit. "Dr. Farris and Wes are old friends. But she was also friends with Jessie Beecham. She was having an affair with Jessie around the time he was murdered."

Brandon wanted to kick himself. He'd been so involved in keeping Willa safe that he hadn't given this case the time and work it needed. Hell. Even though this wasn't his specific case, he was a lawman, and he should have done better. If he had, this investigation might already be over and the danger gone.

He glanced at Willa to let her know he was sorry, but he only saw skepticism in her eyes. Brandon had that same skepticism, but what he couldn't doubt was that Dean appeared completely confident that he was telling the truth.

Brandon would check every detail to make sure he was.

"If Dr. Farris was having an affair with Jessie as you say, then why would she want to help the person who possibly murdered him?" Brandon challenged.

"Hey, I didn't say she was in love with the man. She's been going back and forth between Wes and Jessie for years. She might not have been sleeping with Wes at the time of Jessie's death, but from what I've learned about her, she wouldn't want him to be arrested for a murder rap."

Dean wasn't painting a very good picture of

Dr. Farris. And Cash must have known her background. Yet he'd brought her to that hotel suite to "help" Willa. Maybe the doctor had really come to see just how much Willa remembered. If so, that meant Dr. Farris could have been the one to alert Martin Shore.

"So, will you help me?" Dean asked. But he wasn't looking at Brandon, he was looking at Willa.

"Help you how?" she asked, wanting to know.

"Tell the cops that I had nothing to do with the hostage situation."

She shook her head. "I can't do that. The gunman—"

Brandon caught her arm to stop her from finishing. He didn't want Dean to know Willa had remembered the gunman trying to call him.

"It's time for you to leave," Brandon told the man.

"No." Dean volleyed glances between the two of them. "Not until she agrees to help me."

"She's not agreeing to anything." Brandon didn't wait for the man to concur. He let go of Willa so he could usher Dean out of the building. Brandon used more force than necessary, and he slammed the door in Dean's face and locked it.

Dean shouted out some profanity and threats, but he must have quickly remembered that only minutes earlier, Wes had been in the area. Brandon watched through the sidelight window as Dean scurried across the back parking lot and climbed into a white compact car.

Brandon turned to Willa to tell her they shouldn't stay put much longer, but she spoke before he could.

"I need access to a computer and the internet," she

told him. "I want to search some files and see what I can learn about all the things Dean just told us."

Brandon had a laptop at his house, but now that Wes and God knows who else knew they were in the area, it might not be safe to stay there. At least at the station, he had the two deputies who could back him up in case something went wrong.

"How long will you need?" Brandon asked, checking his watch.

She shook her head. "I'm not sure. I think I remember how to hack into files."

Brandon knew this was illegal, but he didn't care. Right now, he only wanted to get to the truth, and he wanted that truth in the shortest time possible so he could get Willa out of there.

"You can use my office," Brandon told her. "And while you're doing that, I need to make some calls." He had to do some checking on Cash so he could make sure his old friend hadn't betrayed him.

But first things first, he wanted to call the Texas Ranger crime lab in Austin.

After Willa dropped the photo Dean had given them on Brandon's desk, she sat at his computer and started to tap away on the keys. Brandon worked his way through the Ranger organization and contacted Sergeant Egan Caldwell, a Ranger he'd worked with on several cases. It took Brandon nearly fifteen minutes to get through the explanation and his request. He believed there to be a leak in SAPD and he was asking the Rangers to conduct an impartial investigation into the DNA results from Jessie Beecham's murder.

The request and Sergeant Caldwell's agreement

would no doubt cause waves. Now, the trick was to prevent those waves from placing Willa in any more danger.

Brandon made several more calls, searching for someplace to take her. He couldn't very well ask SAPD to provide a safe house, but he didn't have many options.

"I think I might have found something," Willa announced.

Brandon was about to hurry to the computer when he heard the knock at the front door.

"We're sure popular today," Sheila called back to Brandon a moment later. "Got two more visitors. Strangers at that. Should I let them in?"

"Not yet." Brandon drew his gun and started for the front, but he soon saw the two people standing on the other side of the reinforced glass door.

It was Cash and Dr. Farris.

Chapter Twelve

Willa was now certain of one thing. Nearly every one of their suspects knew where Brandon and she were. Martin Shore was the only one yet to make an appearance at Brandon's office, and she prayed he was far away from them.

She watched from the doorway of his office as Brandon "greeted" their latest visitors. Both Dr. Farris and Cash were visibly angry, but so was Brandon. Heck, so was she.

Especially after what she'd just learned about Dr. Farris.

Thank goodness her hacking skills were as sharp as ever. Willa might not remember key incidents of the past two months, but she obviously recalled how to worm her way into someone's personal information.

Now what she needed was some time to dig into the other suspects' computer files. So far they hadn't had much time to do that.

There hadn't been time for much of anything.

They had both showered and changed their clothes before Pete had arrived to pick them up at Brandon's house. Brandon had replaced his jeans with a clean pair and put on a black shirt and leather jacket. Hardly Christmas colors but neither was Willa's cream-colored sweater. She hadn't had anything else clean to wear, which meant she was either going to have to do laundry soon or buy something new. Heaven knows when she would get the chance to do either.

"Let us in," Cash demanded. "It's freezing out here."

It was, and that probably explained why Cash and the doctor were huddled together. Both had their heads lowered, but the sleet was starting to come down.

"Are you two friends again?" Brandon asked Cash and the doctor, not keeping the sarcasm from his voice. "Because just a few hours ago, you thought Dr. Farris here might be supplying bad guys with information about Willa."

The doctor turned that frosty look at Cash. "No. We're not friends. And we didn't arrive together. I had no idea he was coming here until I saw him pull into the parking lot."

"I'm a cop," Cash reminded her. "I have a right to be here." He aimed his attention at Brandon. "Any reason you wouldn't tell me where you were?"

"Yeah. The reason is Martin Shore and his repeated attempts to kill Willa." Brandon kept a tight grip on his weapon, and he didn't move out of the doorway so the pair could fully enter the station.

"I'm trying to stop another attack," Cash insisted. "That's why I've spent the past few hours looking for you. I got your address from the state database, but it wasn't in the GPS. I found the farm road and stopped and asked someone where your place was, but the person wouldn't tell me. He said it would be dangerous for me to try to get to your house anyway because you keep attack dogs."

Good. Brandon would thank all his neighbors first chance he got for keeping the location of his house a secret.

"It's cold," the doctor reminded Brandon. She shoved her hands in her pockets and bobbed on her tiptoes in an attempt to keep warm.

"Then if you want to get warm, my suggestion is talk fast so you can leave fast," Brandon told them, and it earned him more glares from the pair.

Dr. Farris looked past Brandon, and the doctor's gaze met Willa's. She grabbed the photo Dean had given them and walked closer. She kept the picture facing toward her in case Brandon wanted to withhold it for some reason. But she wanted them to see, and more than that, Willa wanted an explanation about why the three had been together.

"You shouldn't have left without speaking to me," Dr. Farris warned her. "The therapy session wasn't over, and I needed to debrief you so you could put all that you remembered in perspective."

Willa stopped next to Brandon. "I'd had all the perspective I could handle for one day. Plus, Shore was in the lobby waiting for us when we left. I don't suppose either of you would know why he was there?"

The doctor and Cash exchanged glances again and then shook their heads. "I have no idea why he was there," Cash insisted. "But maybe it's like Brandon suggested on the phone—Shore could have been following your PDA."

"My PDA was several buildings away in a parked car."

Cash shrugged. "Maybe Shore had already followed you by then. Maybe he saw you go into the hotel."

Willa couldn't totally discount that, but she didn't intend to trust Cash, either.

"You need to come back with me," the doctor insisted. "Or at least let me finish the session."

"Willa's not going anywhere with you," Brandon informed her. He took the photo from Willa and put it right in Cash and the doctor's faces. "Got an explanation for this?"

Well, that got a reaction. The color drained from Dr. Farris's cheeks, and Cash cursed.

"Where did you get that?" Cash demanded.

"A concerned citizen. Now, would you like to tell me what was going on in this meeting?"

"Nothing," the doctor volunteered. "I was duped into being there."

"But Wes and you are old friends," Willa pointed out.

"*Former* friends," the doctor corrected. "I got a call from someone claiming to be Wes's assistant. The person—a man—told me that Wes had proof of who'd killed Jessie Beecham. I went, of course, because I wanted to know who was responsible so I could have the police arrest him. And when I arrived, Cash was there."

"I got a similar call," Cash continued. He stared at the photo. "So did Wes. It didn't take us long to figure out that we'd all been brought there under false pretenses. But we didn't know why someone would want to bring the three of us together." He paused. "Now, we know. It was to get this incriminating photo."

Again, that could be the truth, but Willa was glad Brandon wasn't letting them inside. It did make her wonder, though, if Dean Quinlan had set up the incriminating photo to throw blame off himself.

"Are you sure this meeting wasn't to figure out how to place the blame on the homeless man who's in jail for the murder?" Brandon asked.

Cash opened his mouth to speak, but it took him a few seconds to form the words. The anger tightened and twisted his face. "Brandon, you've got the wrong idea about me. I'm one of the good guys."

"Maybe," Brandon mumbled.

"There's more," Willa started and she glanced at Brandon to make sure it was okay to reveal what she had learned on her computer search. He had no idea what she knew, of course, since there hadn't been time to tell him, but Willa hoped that he would trust her not to spill anything that would only make this worse.

Brandon nodded.

And Willa met the doctor eye to eye. "Dr. Farris, you've come into a rather large sum of money recently."

The doctor placed her hand on her chest, and her mouth dropped open. "How would you know that?" But she shook her head and didn't wait for Willa to answer. "You invaded my privacy. You snooped on me. Well, it doesn't matter. The money was a gift from my grandfather."

"Really?" Willa questioned. "It came in seven different deposits, all just small enough not to alert the IRS. That's not usually the way people give gifts."

Cash and Brandon both gave the doctor a suspicious stare.

Dr. Farris huffed and made an adjustment to the collar of her coat so that it covered the back of her neck. "What? You think that money was some kind of payoff?"

"Was it?" Brandon asked. "Maybe Wes paid you off to keep quiet about him murdering your lover, Jessie Beecham?"

The doctor made a sound of outrage. "I don't have to listen to this. This conversation is over." And with that, she turned and started toward a sleek silver sports car that was parked just up the street.

One down, one to go.

But Cash didn't leave. Instead, his phone rang, and after glancing at the caller ID screen, he took the call. Brandon started to shut the door, but Cash held up his index finger in a wait-a-second gesture. Brandon did wait, but he leaned over and put his mouth to Willa's ear.

"We'll be leaving as soon as I'm done with Cash," he told her.

That didn't surprise Willa, but she had to wonder—where would they go now? Would it be safe enough to return to Brandon's house? Probably not. But then, she wasn't sure it was safe anywhere.

The baby kicked, as if in protest.

Cash ended his call and slapped his phone shut. "You

called the Texas Rangers," he said to Brandon in an accusing tone.

"Yeah, I did," Brandon readily admitted. "I want them to review Jessie Beecham's murder investigation, including the DNA samples."

"Those samples were tested after the hostage incident. They're clean."

"Then you should have no problem with them being tested again."

"You know I do." Cash's jaw was clenched so tightly that Willa was surprised he could manage to speak. "It'll make me look bad in the eyes of my superior officers." He cursed. "Hell, Brandon, you know how this works. Even if those tests hold up—and they will—there'll be questions about how I've handled this case."

Brandon took a step closer. "I need those questions answered. Willa and the baby are in danger, and I thought this was the fastest way to get to the truth."

"You could have come to me!" Cash practically shouted.

Brandon shook his head. "I'm not even sure I can trust you." He held up the picture to remind him of why. "Someone has been leaking info at SAPD, and I want to know who."

"Well, it sure as hell isn't me." Cash groaned and scrubbed his hand over his face. "Come on, we fought together side by side. I deserve the benefit of the doubt."

"No. I can't give you that. Not with Willa's safety at stake. And not until I know for sure who told Martin

Shore the location of the safe house where Willa and I were nearly killed."

Cash's gaze flew to Brandon's. "Dr. Farris. She could be the leak."

Willa didn't intend to look so skeptical, but it certainly seemed as if Cash was saying anything to try to save his own skin. "How would Dr. Farris have had access to the information about the safe house?" she asked.

Cash pulled in a hard breath. "She might have gotten it from my computer."

"What?" Brandon snapped.

"I didn't give her the information," Cash quickly defended himself. "But it's possible she got it when I was away from my desk. She showed up about the time we were making the arrangements for the safe house. She said she had the DVD for the therapy and she wanted to get in touch with Willa. I had to leave my desk for a couple of minutes to see someone, and when I came back, Dr. Farris was in my chair, waiting."

"Waiting?" Willa repeated. "Then what makes you think she accessed the location of the safe house?"

"Because it was on my computer screen." Cash continued to explain even over Brandon's loud groan. "I don't remember leaving the file open. In fact, I could have sworn that I closed it."

Brandon got in his face. "And why are you just telling me this now?"

"Because I forgot about it. I haven't exactly been twiddling my thumbs since then. I've been trying to figure out who's after you."

"I don't want your help figuring that out," Willa let

him know. She lifted her hand so Cash could see that she'd written Trust Brandon Ruiz on her palm. "Your name isn't on there for a reason. So, please, just leave me alone."

She thought Cash might argue with her. But he merely belted out some more harsh profanity, turned and walked away. Brandon immediately shut and locked the door.

"He's either innocent," Willa mumbled, "or he puts on a good show. Which is it?"

Brandon shook his head. "I wish I knew. But I don't regret calling the Rangers. In fact, I want to fax Sergeant Caldwell this photo that Dean Quinlan gave us and tell him it'd be in the best interest of the case to dig into Dr. Farris's financial records."

All of that was good, but a new investigation might take months to complete. She didn't have months. Her baby would arrive in about sixty days. Maybe it was some kind of early nesting instincts, but Willa wanted to be settled and soon.

But where?

And how?

She thought of the cash she had in several safety deposit boxes in San Antonio and Austin. She either had to get to one of them and start out some place new, or...

She had to continue to rely on Brandon.

"What?" Brandon asked, probably noticing the renewed concern on her face.

She stared at him and remembered the kisses. The hot attraction. Willa remembered how much she wanted him.

And how much he was trying to keep his emotional distance from her.

That helped with her decision.

She checked the time. It was too late to make it to San Antonio or Austin before the banks closed, and tomorrow was Christmas. It would be the day after before she could get to her cash.

"On the twenty-sixth, I'll need to go to a bank in San Antonio," Willa told him. "You think you can get me there safely?"

He studied her as if trying to figure out what was going on in her head. And he probably would, too. Brandon seemed to be in tune with that she was thinking.

He clutched her shoulders and looked her in the eye. "I'll protect you both until this is over."

Yes, he would. She didn't doubt that. But this would take a heavy emotional toll on both of them. Because the longer she was with him, the more she wanted him. The more she started to spin a fantasy of them being together to raise this child growing inside her.

Rather than start an argument with him, Willa merely nodded, but she would get to the bank the day after Christmas, and she'd go off on her own again.

And her heart would be broken.

But she would have to deal with that later, after she was sure her baby girl was safe.

"I need to pick up some things from my house," Brandon told her. "Let me send this fax, and we'll get out of here."

She turned, ready to go back to his office, but the sound stopped her. It came in an instant with no warning.

A loud blast shook the building.

Willa gasped and automatically ducked down. However, it wasn't a shot. It took her a moment to realize that there had been an explosion.

She looked out the glass door and saw the flames and the debris in the building directly across the street. Oh, God. She knew that sound and recognized the destruction.

A grenade had gone off.

Chapter Thirteen

"Get down!" Brandon yelled, not just to Willa but also to his two deputies who were still in the building.

Brandon pushed Willa to the floor and aimed his gun, but he had nothing to aim at. The diner on the other side of the street was in flames. Since it had closed early because of the holiday, there was no one inside. He couldn't see anyone milling around, either. That was the good news.

But someone or something had caused that explosion.

"You okay, Brandon?" Pete shouted.

"Yeah." Brandon glanced back at Pete who also had his weapon drawn. By his side, Sheila had done the same. "Call the fire department. I don't want that fire spreading to other businesses on Main Street. But tell them not to approach the area until they get an all-clear from one of us."

Brandon heard Sheila pick up the phone and do as he'd asked.

"There's a hired gun after Willa," he told them when Sheila had finished her call. "His name is Martin Shore.

He's six-two, stocky build and has a military-style haircut. He's armed and dangerous."

"I don't see anybody," Pete relayed, and with his gun pointed toward the burning diner, he inched closer.

"Look harder," Brandon insisted. He whispered for Willa to stay down, and he levered himself up so he could look as well.

There was still no one visible on the street, but that didn't mean the assassin wasn't there.

Because Brandon had his attention fixed on the burning building, he saw the second explosion at the exact moment that he heard it. The blast tore through the fiery debris and what was left of the diner, and it sent a spray of fire and ashes right at them.

"What the hell is going on out there?" Pete grumbled as he dropped to the floor.

Hell was the appropriate word for what Shore was creating out there. The assassin might be trying to scare them or draw them out, and he was tearing up the town to do it. Of course, Brandon had to consider that the next grenade would be launched at the sheriff's office.

"Help me!" someone yelled.

With her breath gusting, Willa looked back at Brandon. "That's Wes Dunbar."

Yeah. And his shout had come from the front door.

"Let me in!" Wes demanded.

Not a chance. Brandon had no idea if Wes and Shore were partners in crime or if these latest explosions were a result of Wes working alone. And he didn't have time to find out.

"Are we going out there to make sure we don't have any injuries on our hands?" Sheila asked.

That would be standard procedure. It would also be procedure to identify the assailant's location and stop him from doing any more harm.

But Brandon looked down at Willa.

She was shaking and pale, obviously terrified. She had her hands over her belly. He had to try to end this as quickly as possible and get her out of there.

"Call the sheriff over in LaMesa Springs and have him send us some backup," Brandon instructed his deputies.

LaMesa was the town nearest to them, but it was still a good half hour away. By the time backup arrived, it could be too late. Shore might blow up the entire town to get to Willa.

"Sheriff Tanner and his deputy are on their way," Sheila relayed several moments later.

Another blast rattled the windows and sent them all ducking for cover. Outside, Wes banged on the door again and yelled for help.

"The SOB blew up the feed store," Pete spat out.

That did it. Brandon knew this wouldn't end until he stopped it. He got up from the floor despite the fact Willa was trying to pull him back down.

"Martin Shore is a hit man," she reminded him. "The minute you step outside, he'll try to kill you."

That was probably true, but if Shore managed to get close enough to the sheriff's office, he'd kill them all. Or try anyway.

"Brandon, I don't usually argue with what you plan on doing, but I gotta argue with you now," Pete said.

He glanced at Willa. "If this hired gun is after her like you say, then this is where he's headed. It'd be best if Sheila and I go out back and see if we can spot him."

"And maybe kill him," Sheila added.

Pete nodded. "And if he gets through us, at least you'll be here to protect her. I've got no stomach for a pregnant woman being at the mercy of a man who likes to toss grenades. Stay here, boss. And protect that woman and her baby."

Brandon wanted to argue. He wanted it to be him who went out the door and put his life on the line. That was actually his comfort zone. But protecting Willa and the child was also his duty, and they had to come first. Because Pete was right—Shore was almost certainly headed this way.

Brandon finally nodded, giving his deputies the okay.

"We're going out back," Sheila said without hesitation. "If I get a shot at him, I'm taking it."

Good. Because Sheila had solid aim, better than Pete's, and Brandon trusted her to do her job.

"What should we do about the guy yelling out front?" Pete asked.

"Steer clear of him," Brandon warned. "He could be in on this."

Pete nodded, and after Sheila and he put on their heavy jackets, they headed for the back door. Brandon followed them and watched as they made their exit, locking the door behind them. Shore wouldn't be able to get in that way without Brandon hearing him, but the place had eight windows in all. Each had wire mesh running through the glass so that would make it harder for anyone to break in.

Unless Shore bashed through one of them with a grenade.

"Should we stay here or go to your office?" Willa asked.

Brandon glanced around, trying to determine the best place for them to make their stand. Behind the reception desk might be their safest bet. He could see both the front and back doors from that position, and the large reinforced window at the front allowed him to watch what was happening on Main Street. And right now what was happening was the two fires.

He caught the movement from the corner of his eye and automatically shifted his gun in that direction. It had come from the right of the burning diner.

Brandon tried to pick through the thick black smoke to see if it was Shore. But it wasn't. It was a tall man wearing a suit, and Brandon didn't recognize him.

"Over here!" Wes yelled. And the suited man responded by waving. It was Wes's driver.

But what the heck were they still doing in town? Wes had stormed out of his office at least twenty minutes earlier and should have been long gone by now.

"I'm driving over there to get you," the man called out to Wes. He headed for his car.

But he didn't get far.

Something must have alerted him because he swung around and took aim at the other side of the car. In the same motion, he dropped, using the vehicle for cover.

Beneath him, Willa waited, and he could feel her pulse in every part of his body.

They didn't have to wait long.

Brandon saw the movement. So slight. At first, he thought it was a swirl of black smoke. But then he saw the man's hand.

And the gun he carried.

The man stepped out from the cover of the building near Wes's car, and he didn't take aim at the driver who was now on the ground.

He took aim at the window of the sheriff's office.

Right at Brandon.

And he fired.

BRANDON PUSHED HER DOWN a split-second before Willa heard something slam into the window of the sheriff's office. She had no doubt that it was a bullet. She also had no doubt about who had fired it.

Martin Shore.

She'd caught just a glimpse of the assassin before Brandon had maneuvered her out of the semi-crouching position and flat on the floor. Well, as flat as she could manage. She was on her side with her hands covering her belly.

There was another thick blast, no doubt from another shot, but she didn't hear the sound of breaking glass. Maybe that meant the reinforced steel webbing was holding the window in place. It probably wouldn't hold for long, especially since Shore fired another shot.

She no longer heard Wes's frantic shouts for them to let him in. Maybe the man had wised up and gotten away from there.

Or maybe Shore had already killed him.

Until this attack, she had thought that maybe Wes

had hired Shore to come after her, but after hearing Wes's reaction to the explosion, either he was extremely good at faking fear, or he was an innocent bystander in all of this.

Another bullet slammed into the window, and this time she did hear the glass crashing to the floor. She also felt the cold air start to spill into the building. Brandon didn't return fire. Maybe that's because he would have to fire through the window as well, and he perhaps didn't want to create an opening that Shore could use to shoot at them.

"Let's go," Brandon told her. "But stay down."

She did stay down. He didn't. Brandon rushed them to his office and got her inside, but instead of coming in with her, he stood in the hallway and took aim.

He was right in the line of fire.

There was another shot.

Then, another.

Where were the deputies? Why couldn't they get to Shore and stop him?

Her heart was pounding now, and Willa tried to force herself to calm down. This fear and anxiety might hurt the baby. But she couldn't discount the fact that all of them might die here today. And for what? To cover up what she'd been forced to do while she had been a hostage?

Or was something else going on here?

Brandon had positioned her on the side of his desk, but she could still see out the single window in the center of the wall. Willa kept watch, but she knew that Shore was still at the front because she could hear his shots.

"Stay down," Brandon told her.

And he fired.

That meant Shore had either destroyed the window or was maybe already inside.

She wanted to tell Brandon to get down as well and to be careful, but the movement outside the window caught her attention. It wasn't the deputies. Or Martin Shore.

It was Dean Quinlan.

He didn't appear to be armed, but he had his back pressed to the building next to them. What the heck was he doing out there?

"Brandon," she warned. "Dean's outside."

He stepped back into his office, and his gaze slashed to the window. He didn't take aim at the man but instead kept his gun in the direction of the last shot that had been fired.

She heard the sound of more breaking glass, followed by a heavy thud. Someone was trying to kick in the door.

Oh, God.

Shore was breaking in.

Willa spotted more movement outside the window. It was Pete, the deputy, and he went to Dean and pushed the man to the ground. Pete, too, kept his weapon aimed in the direction of the front of the building. Maybe, just maybe, Pete could get off a shot and stop Shore.

At least that's what she thought until she heard the next bullet.

It didn't come into the building but rather the narrow alley where Dean and Pete were. Pete dropped to the ground as well, but Willa couldn't tell if he'd been hit.

Brandon slammed his door and caught her shoulder to move her deeper into the room, next to a metal filing cabinet. Willa no longer had a clear view of Dean and Pete, but she did see something else.

"That's Wes's driver," she told Brandon.

The man came out from across the street and he had a gun in his hand. He took aim but she couldn't tell who or what he was aiming at.

Pete got back to his feet as well and aimed in the same direction as Wes's driver.

Everything seemed to happen at once. She heard the front door crack and give way. Brandon threw open his own office door and stepped into the hall, ready to kill the intruder.

Willa heard herself call out to him, but her words were drowned out by the sound of the shots. There seemed to be so many of them, all coming from different directions, and the combined blast was deafening.

She closed her eyes for just a second and prayed that Brandon hadn't been hurt.

When she looked out, Brandon was still standing. Thank God. He had his gun pointed toward the front door. So did Wes's driver. And neither man was moving.

"He's down!" Pete shouted.

Did Pete mean Shore? Relief flooded through her, but Willa reminded herself that he could have meant someone else. There had been a lot of shots fired in the past thirty seconds, and there were other people outside, not just Shore.

She waited with her breath held.

"You okay, boss?" Sheila called out.

Brandon glanced at Willa first. "We're okay," he answered.

Willa tried to see what was going on, but everyone had left the alley. Brandon moved too and went toward the front of the station.

She followed him, terrified of what she might see and that Shore might still be standing out there ready to do what he had been hired to do.

The door was wide open, the wind battering it against the wall, and there were massive gaping holes in what was left of the window. She spotted Wes across the street. He was behind his driver. Or maybe a better word for the man would be *bodyguard* because that's what he seemed to be doing—protecting Wes. He had Wes positioned behind him as Brandon had her.

They inched closer, but Brandon didn't lower his gun.

Willa saw Pete and Dean to the right. Sheila was on the left. Both deputies had their weapons trained as well, but they were definitely converging toward the front door.

She soon realized why.

There was a pool of blood on the small concrete step directly in front of the door, and next to that pool lay Martin Shore.

"I had to shoot him," Wes's driver confessed. "He was about to put a bullet in your deputy."

Brandon stooped down and put his fingers to Shore's neck. Checking for a pulse. But Willa knew he wouldn't find one. Shore's blank eyes were fixed on the dull winter sky, and there was no life left in him.

No life and no breath.

And that meant he couldn't tell them who had hired him to kill her.

This wasn't over.

Chapter Fourteen

Brandon couldn't get his mind to slow down. It was racing with the images and sounds of the latest attack. He could still hear the shots slamming through the glass, and the tremble of Willa's body.

And see the fear on her face.

Those were images that would stay with him for a lifetime.

Once again, she could have easily died, thanks to Martin Shore. And once again, Brandon hadn't been able to prevent her from being at the center of an attack.

His body seemed to be trying to keep up with his racing mind. He put himself on autopilot and tied up what loose ends he could at his office, but he was thankful when the neighboring sheriff, Beck Tanner, and his deputies agreed to take over the investigation so that Brandon could get Willa out of there. That couldn't have happened soon enough. He wanted the baby and her far away from the bullet holes, Martin Shore's dead body and especially away from the person who was responsible for sending Shore after her.

The problem was, Brandon still didn't know who that person was.

Even though Shore was dead and his body was on the way to the county morgue, they didn't know who had hired him.

And might never know.

He certainly couldn't eliminate any of their four suspects. Dean, Wes, Cash and Dr. Farris had all been in the area. And, yes, Wes's man had been the one to shoot and kill Shore, but Wes could have ordered him to do that so he could save his own butt. If Wes thought that Shore was about to be captured and taken into custody, he wouldn't have wanted to risk having the man spill his guts. No. Wes would have told his man to take Shore out.

That thought only caused him and his mind to race more, and when Brandon glanced down at the speedometer, he realized he was going a good twenty miles over the speed limit. Not a bright idea, since the sleet was making the roads slick. Worse, Willa had a white-knuckle grip on the armrest.

"Sorry," he mumbled. And he eased up on the accelerator a bit. Still, he didn't dawdle.

"Don't be. I'm not exactly anxious to be out in the open like this."

Yeah. He knew what she meant. They were literally out in the sticks, nearly eight miles from town and the chaos he'd left there, but Brandon knew that chaos had a way of following them. That's why he had continued to check his rearview mirror throughout the drive.

"We can't stay at my house tonight," he reminded her.

And soon, very soon, he'd need to ditch the car since

it was the one Pete had used to pick them up earlier. Someone could recognize it. Unfortunately, it was the sheriff department's only vehicle that hadn't been hit with bullets in the attack.

"So where will we go?" she asked, checking the side mirror as well.

Brandon had considered several possibilities—including a drive back into Austin or San Antonio. The problem with that was the icy roads, and it was getting late. The sun was already close to setting, and that would drop the temperatures even farther. He didn't want to risk getting into an accident.

Plus, there was no one he truly trusted in either of those places.

If they went to either city, they would have to check into a hotel, and while he had the cash stashed at home to do that, paying with cash might alert a curious desk clerk who might in turn alert the police. Brandon figured if Wes had heard about the attacks on Willa, then it had likely been on the news. This latest attack and Shore's death would be reported as well, and the press would be able to come up with photos. Their faces could be plastered on the pages of every newspaper in the state.

And that brought him back to their temporary sleeping arrangements.

"There's a fishing cabin on the back part of my property," he told her. He turned on the road that led to his house, and he saw the dogs race out to greet them. "There's no electricity, but I do have a generator. We can stay there tonight and then figure out tomorrow where we should go."

"Or you could just drop me off somewhere and put some distance between us." She said it so softly that it took a moment to sink in.

"You think I'd leave you?" He hadn't intended to sound so angry, but damn it, that riled him.

"I think it would be smart for you to do that. Right now, the person who hired Shore is looking for *us*. As in the *two* of us. If we split up, he or she will be looking only for me." She shook her head. "And we both know it's me they're really after."

Brandon brought the car to a stop, not in front of his house, but he parked inside the garage, and he used the remote control to shut the door. While it ground to a close, he turned in the seat to face her. "Let's get something straight. I'm not leaving you." Well, not until he was positive she was safe.

The look in her eyes told him that she understood that last unspoken part.

He cursed and reached for the car door. "Come in with me to get some things."

Because he sure didn't want her waiting in the car alone. It had been chilly before, but it was bitterly cold now, and that along with the possible danger caused them to rush inside. He locked the door and set the security system even though he only planned to be there for a half hour or so.

"Don't turn on the lights, but if you want to wash up, you'd better do it here," Brandon let her know. He tried to take the anger out of his voice but failed. Hell. She had actually thought she could talk him into dumping her so he could save himself. "There won't be any hot water at the cabin."

No hot water. No heat other than the fireplace. No bed, just a single army-style cot. And no comforts of home. It wouldn't be an ideal place to spend what was left of Christmas Eve.

He grabbed his old duffel bag and headed to the linen closet so he could grab some bedding. The place wasn't exactly pitch dark, yet, but he had a little trouble locating the thermal blankets. When he finally got them, he shoved them into the bag and then started for the kitchen.

Willa stepped out in front of him.

"You're mad at me," she said, "but you have to admit I'm sort of like Typhoid Mary right now. There really is no reason for both of us to be in danger."

Oh, yes, there was. Brandon put his hand on her stomach to remind her. He'd intended for it to be a quick touch, but he held it there.

There was just enough light left that he could see her face. Willa stood there looking at him, and her right eyebrow lifted as if questioning him as to what he was about to do.

Brandon had no idea.

He just knew that touching Willa wasn't a good idea. Still, even with the danger and his anger, he didn't stop and didn't pull back. They both seemed to be waiting to see what would happen next.

And what happened next was that he snapped his arm around her, pulled her to him and kissed her. He wasn't gentle. He didn't give her a chance to change her mind and pull away. Brandon just took what was right there in front of him.

Maybe he meant this as some kind of reassurance

that he would be there for her. But Brandon cursed himself. This didn't have anything to do with reassurances. He'd been burning to kiss Willa since their last kissing session had ended. He wanted her, and there was no logical explanation for it other than she got him hot.

She curved her hand around the back of his neck and moved as close as she could get. Because of the pregnancy, they weren't exactly body to body, but they were plenty close enough for Brandon to deepen the kiss. He didn't taste the fear or the adrenaline from the attack.

He only tasted Willa.

Man.

That taste went straight through him.

Brandon realized he was trying to get even closer to her when Willa's back hit the wall. That stopped him a moment because he wanted to make sure he wasn't being too rough with her. But Willa merely latched on to a handful of his shirt and pulled him right back to her.

The kiss got even hotter.

They couldn't keep this up. Soon, very soon, their bodies would demand more. They would demand sex. And Brandon knew he had to try to keep a clear head. Plus, having sex with Willa wouldn't be fair since they would no doubt be going their separate ways.

Or would they?

Maybe the scalding kisses were melting his brain because Brandon realized they couldn't entirely go their separate ways.

Hell.

When had that happened?

When had he decided that he would want to see this baby after she was born?

He pulled back again, blinked. And he tried to gather the strength to stop this so he could think. But he saw Willa again. Her mouth was slightly swollen from the hard kisses, and her breath was fast and thin. But that wasn't a "let's stop" look in her eyes.

No way.

Those heavy-lidded eyes were sending out an invitation that his body had no trouble understanding. She wanted to have sex with him and she wanted it now.

Brandon wanted that, too, and there was no amount of willpower that would stop him from taking her mouth again. Willa made a sound of relief. Maybe even victory. And she melted into the kiss.

Her arms went around him, and she fought to get closer. Hard to do but not impossible. Brandon slid his hand between them and shoved up her sweater so he could touch her breasts. She was perfect. Full and round. He'd always been a sucker for a curvy woman, and the pregnancy had obviously left Willa's breasts ripe for the touching.

So, that's what Brandon did.

He shoved down the cups of her bra and circled her nipples with his fingers. Willa obviously approved because she made more of those sounds of pleasure and relief.

Brandon felt no relief. Every touch was like fire to his blood, and he felt that fire course through him. He was already hard and ready for her, but that need skyrocketed when he lowered his head and took her right nipple into his mouth.

"Yes," she mumbled.

That *yes* slammed through him as much as the kisses had done. Maybe more. His body began to demand that he do something about the powder keg that was building inside him.

His mouth went back to hers for a hard, punishing kiss, and he shoved his hand into the waist of her pants and into her panties.

He found her, hot and wet, and he groaned because that wouldn't help any shred of resolve he had left. No. It told him what he already knew.

That he was going to have her.

Here and now.

It didn't have to make sense. It didn't even have to be right. But it would happen.

Brandon scooped Willa up into his arms and headed for the bedroom.

WILLA WAS AWARE THAT she was moving, but she didn't care where Brandon was taking her. She only cared about one thing—finally making love with Brandon.

She'd been burning for him since the moment she laid eyes on him. Lust at first sight. But it seemed to be a lot more than just lust. She'd never felt this intensity. Never wanted a man more than her next breath.

However, Brandon seemed to have set a new benchmark.

Even though he hurried to the bedroom, he was gentle when he lay her on the bed. The old-fashioned feather mattress swelled around her, cocooning her in its softness. Brandon followed on top of her, using his forearms to keep his weight from bearing down on her belly. He wasn't soft. He was all sinew and muscle.

All man.

He continued to kiss her, and he set fires wherever his mouth touched her. On her neck. On the tops of her breasts. He kissed her through the fabric of her top. At first. But she wanted his lips and breath on her skin so Willa fought to shove up her top and open her bra.

Brandon took her exactly the way she wanted to be taken.

This foreplay was sweet torture, but the kisses only made her want more.

Since it would almost certainly take some maneuvering for them to have more, Willa turned, shifting their positions so that she was on top. Her sweater had to go so she peeled off both it and her bra and tossed them aside.

In the back of her mind, she considered that she probably didn't look very sexy, but that didn't seem to bother Brandon. He pushed down her stretchy pants, exposing her belly and giving him access to her panties.

He touched her again. Watched her. And while Willa straddled him, she watched him, too. Brandon was lost in the fire, his eyes hot with need. And that need only fueled hers. He had on too many clothes for sex, and she wanted him naked.

His coat came off easily, but she struggled with his holster and gun. Brandon stopped his own attempts to get her out of her pants so he could help. His hands and fingers that had been so clever touching her now seemed rushed and awkward. Willa felt awkward and cursed when she couldn't get his jeans unzipped.

Brandon placed his hand over hers, sliding down the zipper so that Willa could touch him the way he had touched her. Even though the lights were off, she could still see his face. She could see what her touch did to him, and even though she hadn't thought it possible, she burned even hotter for him.

He was clearly ready for sex so Willa saw no reason to wait. She couldn't wait. Her mind and body were racing, pushing her toward the relief that suddenly felt as necessary as life itself.

His hands were rushed again. So was his breath. His breath gusted, his chest pumping as if starved for air. Brandon got her pants and panties off, and he didn't waste even a second of time.

Neither did Willa.

Since she was still straddling him, she was in the perfect position to move this to the next level. She lowered herself, taking him into her body. Inch by inch. Until she had him fully inside her.

The pleasure blurred her vision and sent her heart racing.

Over the past two days, her heart had been doing a lot of racing, but for the first time, it was due to pleasure and not fear. And there was no doubt about it—this was pleasure in its purest form.

She moved. Brandon did, too. He caught her hips to set the rhythm of the strokes inside her. It was too fast. Too frantic. Too intense to last. But Willa wasn't interested in prolonging this. Not this time, anyway. Maybe some other time they could have a long leisurely afternoon of lovemaking. But this time, she needed him too much to want anything but completion.

Brandon didn't try to slow things, either. He continued to take them both to the only place they wanted to go.

Willa locked gazes with him as their bodies found the perfect rhythm and pace to create exactly what they needed. He moved faster. Harder. The grip he had on her hips tightened and everything honed in on that one moment. That one prize that was just seconds within their reach.

"Do something about this," she heard herself mumble.

Brandon did something about it all right. He lifted his hips, pulling her down onto him for one last hard penetrating stroke.

And that was it.

That was all it took.

It was exactly what she needed to go spinning over the edge. Her body closed around him, as he pulled her to him. Close and tight in his arms.

With her heartbeat echoing in her ears and her breath filling the room, she still heard him. She heard what he said at the moment of his surrender.

Brandon whispered her name.

Chapter Fifteen

Even though Brandon's body wanted to stay put with Willa in his arms, the sane and logical part of his brain kicked in. Thank goodness. Because it just wasn't a smart idea for them to linger there and enjoy the moment.

And what a moment.

Later, and probably a lot sooner than he wanted, he would regret this. The timing was all wrong.

Hell.

The sex itself was wrong, too.

He shouldn't have taken Willa as if he had a right to do that. He had no rights. He'd given her no hope of a future, only the pity story of his biological father.

All of that seemed, well, pointless right now. But that was probably because he'd just had the best sex of his life. His body wanted to have her all over again. His body wanted him to stay inside her and stare up at her beautiful face.

But thankfully, his brain reminded him of the danger.

Brandon eased her off him, and Willa slumped onto the mattress. She was obviously trying to catch her breath, and he wondered if this had been too much for her. He didn't know anything about having sex with a pregnant woman.

"Are you okay?" he asked.

She smiled, maybe to soothe the alarm on his face and in his voice, and she slid her hand around the back of his neck to pull him to her for a kiss. It wasn't a peck. It was the kiss from a woman who was definitely interested in round two. Because that couldn't happen—well, not right now anyway—Brandon ended the mouth-to-mouth contact and got up from the bed so he could dress.

"We have to leave," he reminded her.

Willa groaned, and that sound went right through him. Resisting Willa was next to impossible. Still, he resisted. And Brandon put on his shorts and jeans before his body talked him into getting back in that bed with her.

She got up, too, and the smile didn't leave her face while she dressed. Well, it didn't until she caught him staring at her belly.

"Sorry," she mumbled, quickly pulling on her pants. "Sometimes, I forget just how big I am."

"You're not *big,* you're pregnant. You're supposed to be this size."

And because he thought they both could use it, he slid his hand over her stomach, over the baby, and he kissed her. Like Willa's kiss, it wasn't a peck, either. It turned hot way too fast, but Brandon ended it before it became the start of more mind-blowing foreplay.

"After what just happened, you must know I'm attracted to you," he said against her mouth.

"Even with the pregnant belly?" she questioned.

Especially with the pregnant belly. But since that made him sound like some kind of pervert, Brandon just settled for a nod.

"I need to pack us some food," he hurriedly added. *Keep your mind on the task and get your hands off Willa.* "When we leave tomorrow, there might not be any stores or restaurants open."

He put his holster and jacket back on and headed to the kitchen. Willa could probably use a few minutes alone anyway. To freshen up.

To deal with her regrets.

Brandon was sure she would have them eventually. After all, he might be her baby's father, but he had more baggage than she needed.

He grabbed a plastic bag from beneath the sink and filled it with some granola bars, apples and bottled water. It was hardly the makings of a Christmas dinner, but he hadn't planned on holiday food. If things had been normal, he would have settled for a turkey sandwich while covering the office so that Pete and Sheila could spend the day with their families.

Families.

That word caused him to take a deep breath. Soon, very soon, he had to work out what that meant to him as far as Willa and the baby were concerned.

While he slapped together two turkey sandwiches, Brandon glanced out the kitchen window above the sink. The sun had just set, but he could see and hear the sleet pinging against the glass. It would be a slow, hazardous drive out to the cabin, but there was no way he would make Willa walk the two-plus miles in this weather.

He heard a sound and first thought it was the rustling of the trees in the wind, but he looked closer. Despite the sleet, the oaks near the house were practically still.

An uneasy feeling went through him, and he set the bread aside so he could get a better look. However, he stepped back from the window. Far back and kept in the shadows. And he waited.

Brandon saw it then.

The car.

It was just up the road, probably no more than a hundred yards from the house. There were no headlights, and the car was dark colored. With the clouds covering the moon, he might not have spotted it at all if hadn't been for the vehicle's parking lights.

His stomach went to his knees.

This couldn't be good. If Sheila, Pete or any of the other townsfolk were coming to see him in this weather, they wouldn't have turned off their headlights. No. There was only one reason to do that.

So the driver could sneak up on them.

"Willa?" Brandon softly called out to her. He tried to keep his voice calm while he kept an eye on the car. It was definitely moving closer, inching along at a snail's pace.

But eventually the driver would arrive at the house.

Brandon was betting whoever that driver was, he or she would be up to no good.

"Yes?" Willa answered.

He heard her footsteps leading out of the bedroom and toward the kitchen. But what he didn't hear were the dogs. If anyone or anything had gotten close to the house, Butch and Sundance would have alerted him. They'd be barking their heads off.

So, why hadn't his dogs sounded the alarm?

Brandon wasn't sure he wanted to know the answer to that.

"Are we ready?" Willa asked, walking into the kitchen. But she froze the moment she saw Brandon. That was probably because he'd drawn his gun. "What's wrong?"

He really hated to tell her this. She'd already been through too much. But he couldn't exactly keep this from her, either. "Someone's out there."

She gasped, hurried to him and followed his gaze out the window. "Who is it?"

Brandon shook his head. "It's my guess that the driver isn't paying a friendly visit."

"Oh, God." And she frantically started looking around the kitchen.

For a moment Brandon thought she might on the verge of panicking, but he soon realized she was looking for a knife. She found one in the drawer and pulled it out.

"There's a gun on top of the fridge," he let her know. And while he didn't like the idea of Willa being armed, he didn't like the alternative any better.

Besides, things could turn ugly fast, and she might need to defend herself.

She fished around on the fridge and came up with the Smith & Wesson. It was loaded, and thankfully she treated it that way. She kept it pointed toward the floor.

"Where are the dogs?" she asked.

Brandon had to shake his head again. "I didn't hear any gunshots," he added. Though Willa likely knew that someone could have used a silencer.

It cut at Brandon's heart to think of someone harming his pets, but right now he had to put all his focus on protecting Willa.

"Check the security system panel by the front door and make sure the red light is on," he told Willa. "And stay away from the windows."

She scurried away and Brandon kept watch. The car came even closer but stopped just on the other side of his mailbox. The doors didn't open, and he saw no signs of the driver trying to exit.

It was possible that the person didn't know they were inside. After all, their car was parked in the garage with the door down, and they hadn't turned on any lights. Maybe, just maybe, if he could hide with Willa, the driver would assume the place was empty and leave.

Brandon wasn't sure he wanted that to happen. Part of him wanted to confront this SOB who could be responsible for hiring Shore to come after Willa. But if he could avoid a gunfight with Willa around, then that had to be his first option. No bullets meant Willa and the baby would be safe for another day.

Until the next confrontation.

"The red light is on, and the system is armed," Willa said, coming back into the room. "What do we do now?"

It was risky to stay inside because the person could

try to blow up the house. But it would be an even bigger risk to go outside.

Brandon considered the garage. They could get in the car and wait as they had at the safe house. But that wasn't without risks, either, especially since he would have to disarm the security system for them to go through the mudroom door and into the garage. Plus, there was a door at the back of the garage that led to the yard. He was certain he had locked it, but locks could be easily broken.

"For now, we'll wait here, inside," he whispered.

Brandon moved Willa to the side of the fridge and positioned himself in front of her. They were now out of range of the window, but he could see the back door, and if he peered around the fridge, he could see the front one as well. Thankfully, with the exception of the exterior garage, all the doors and windows were wired with the security system so it should go off if someone tried to break in.

If that happened, they would have to go with Plan B.

He would try to get Willa to the garage so he could take down this person who was hell-bent on trying to kill them.

Behind him, he could hear Willa's shallow breathing, but that, the sleet and the hum of the fridge were the only sounds in the room. Maybe that's why it wasn't hard for him to hear the car door. It was slight, as if someone was trying to ease it shut, but Brandon still heard it.

He braced himself for whatever was going to happen next. At best, the person might just leave or there'd be a knock at the door. Maybe it was someone lost and having car trouble.

But Brandon didn't think this was an "at best" kind of situation.

The seconds crawled by, and Brandon continued to wait. There were no more sounds of car doors. Not even any footsteps.

Still, he didn't relax.

Good thing, too.

The sound of the shot blasted through the house.

WILLA CHOKED BACK A GASP and took aim in case she had to return fire. But Brandon obviously didn't want her to do that because he pushed her even farther back so that she was against the wall.

With him in front of her.

Protecting her, again.

How many more times was he going to have to put himself in danger like this?

If she hadn't been pregnant, if she had only herself to worry about, Willa would have considered making her own stand. She was exhausted and spent from these attacks, and one way or another, she just wanted them to be over. But she couldn't just step out from cover. She had to think of her baby girl.

Brandon took his cell from his pocket and passed it back to her. "Call Pete. His is the first number."

Though her hands were shaking and she was trying to keep a firm hold on the gun, Willa made it to his list of recent calls and pressed the call button. She held her breath and waited for Pete to answer. She also waited for another sound from their attacker.

But nothing.

Not from their attacker. Nor from Pete. He didn't answer the call, and it went to voice mail.

"Pete didn't answer," she whispered, automatically moving on to Sheila's number who was next on the phone list. Willa tried it as well, but there wasn't an answer from Sheila, either.

Something was wrong. Even though it was Christmas Eve, one of them should have answered.

And why hadn't the dogs barked? As frightened as Willa was of them, she wished the Dobermans were there to protect them. They'd need all the help they could get.

"Sheila didn't answer?" Brandon asked, his voice barely audible.

"No. Should I try anyone else?" But as she was asking, she looked at the list of names and numbers. Since this was his prepaid cell, it obviously didn't include his normal list of contacts. With the exception of Cash, there wasn't anyone else, and they obviously couldn't call him.

Or anyone else in SAPD.

There was another shot and, while Willa had thought she was prepared to hear it, the sound still sent a stab of fear through her. Still, she wouldn't let that fear immobilize her. She had a gun, and even though she wasn't sure she knew how to use it, that wouldn't stop her.

"He's shooting at the lock on the front door," Brandon mumbled.

So that explained why there'd been no sound of breaking glass. And there were no indications of the door opening, either. That was something at least. The person hadn't actually managed to get inside.

So, who was out there?

Cash, maybe. Or Wes, Dr. Farris or even Dean. All of them had motive to keep her silent, and it was entirely possible that one or more of them had teamed up against Brandon and her. All four of them potentially had a lot to lose if she ended up testifying about what had gone on in that lab the day of the hostage incident.

Of course, she had to stay alive to be able to testify.

"Call nine-one-one," he instructed. "Ask for help from the county sheriff's office over in Saddle Springs."

God knows how far away that was, but they needed some kind of backup. She quickly pressed in the numbers, and the dispatcher answered on the first ring.

"I'm Willa Marks," she told the dispatcher. And then she realized she didn't have the address. "I'm at Sheriff Brandon Ruiz's residence near Crockett Creek, and we have an intruder. Send someone immediately."

Since she didn't want her voice to give away her location to the person trying to break in, Willa didn't hang up, but she didn't say anything else.

There was another shot, and this one was different from the other two. It sounded as if the bullet had smacked against something metal.

Maybe the lock? Or maybe it was just the brass doorknob.

The emergency dispatcher continued to talk, asking Willa for details about what was going on. Because the questions were coming from the other end of the line, they weren't loud. But they could still be heard. Willa closed the phone and hoped the dispatcher wouldn't have any trouble relaying the request for immediate help.

Willa heard the sound then. A slight creaking noise. She thought it might have come from the hinges on the door, but she prayed she was wrong.

But she wasn't.

Seconds later, she felt the cold winter air slice through the kitchen.

Oh, God.

Someone had opened the front door.

Chapter Sixteen

Brandon didn't take the time to curse himself for staying too long at his house. But he would do that later. Right now though, he apparently had a fight on his hands.

He eased a fraction away from the fridge so he could get a better look at the front door.

It was open.

He didn't see an intruder and didn't hear footsteps so that could mean the person was lurking on the porch. Bullets could easily come through the window and make their way to Willa and the baby.

Who was out there?

Who was doing this to them?

Brandon desperately wanted to know, but he didn't want that knowledge at Willa's expense. Nor did he want to start a gun battle. Right now, his best bet was to wait. To listen. And to try to get off the shot that would put an end to this.

He glanced back at Willa to make sure she was okay. She looked scared but determined, and she still had hold of the gun she'd taken from the top of the fridge. Good. Because he might need her help.

Finally, he heard the footsteps. It was hard to tell because of the wind howling, but he was pretty sure the intruder was still on the porch. For now, anyway. Those footsteps seemed to be leading straight into the house.

Brandon got ready, and took aim at the front door. He wouldn't have but a split second to identify the person and then shoot, and he couldn't risk not getting off the first shot.

He heard another step. Then, another. But he also heard something else.

A car engine.

He tried turning his ear to the sound, but he couldn't figure out if it was coming from the intruder's vehicle or if someone else had just driven up.

Hell.

He hoped this SOB hadn't brought an accomplice.

Brandon spotted the movement in the doorway, and his finger tightened just slightly on the trigger. He was ready. Too ready. Every muscle and nerve in his body was primed for the fight, but the intruder didn't show his face. He stayed there, in the shadows.

Waiting for Brandon to make the first move.

That wouldn't happen. He had Willa in a protected position right now, and he wasn't going to change that unless it was absolutely necessary.

The seconds ticked off again, but there were no more footsteps. No sounds of a car engine, either. Just the brutal wind and the central heating that had kicked in.

Brandon definitely felt the chill in the air, and behind him, Willa started to shake. Her teeth weren't chattering, yet, but it was close. It hadn't taken but a couple of minutes for the inside temperature to plunge, and with the front door wide open, there was no way the heat could neutralize all that cold air gushing in.

Of course, the intruder was out in the cold, too, and Brandon hoped like the devil that it affected the person's aim and judgment.

There was no movement. No warning. Definitely no footsteps. And even though Brandon was ready for an attack, the sound still surprised him.

A bullet came through the living room window.

The sound blasted through the entire house. So did the shattering glass. The bullet slammed into the kitchen wall by the sink. Not exactly close to Willa and him. A good six feet away. But it was close enough for Brandon to know he had to return fire.

He came out from cover and sent a shot right back through the front window.

Brandon didn't stay in the open. He couldn't. He had to move back into place so that he would be in front of Willa. And once he was there, he waited, praying he'd managed to shoot the intruder.

But there was no indication of that.

Definitely no moan of pain. No body dropping to the porch.

Several seconds later, another shot came roaring into the kitchen. There was no six feet of space this time. The shot came damn close to the fridge.

The third shot came even closer.

"Stay down," he whispered to Willa. Brandon didn't leave cover, but he sent two shots of his own right back at their attacker.

Glass spewed from what was left of the window, but that didn't slow the assault. More bullets came, each of them tearing through his house and coming right at them.

Brandon had no choice but to pull Willa to the floor.

The new position took him out of firing range since there was furniture in between his line of sight and the window. But that same furniture was in the way of the shooter as well. Brandon hoped it would be enough to keep Willa safe.

More bullets came. Four of them. Each were thick blasts that rocketed his adrenaline and put him in fight-or-flight mode. Unfortunately, he needed to take the flight option because of Willa. This person obviously wasn't going to come out in the open so that Brandon would have a clean shot, and this guy wasn't worried about running out of ammunition.

Brandon was.

He couldn't go bullet for bullet in this fight.

"Stay low on the floor," he whispered to Willa. "We're going to the garage."

Yes, it was a risk, but at this point, staying put seemed the biggest risk of all.

Brandon kept himself positioned in front of her, and Willa crawled to the other side of the fridge. He fired another bullet at their attacker and hoped the single shot would buy them a few seconds of time.

It worked.

The person didn't fire any other shots until Willa was near the mudroom door that led out to the garage. Brandon wasn't quite so lucky though. The shot came right at him, and even though he was low on the floor as well, the bullet sliced through the sleeve of his jacket. Well, hopefully it was just the sleeve. He didn't have time to look and see if the bullet had grazed him.

He hurried, trying to get Willa away from the kitchen window. Even though the attacker would have to run from the porch to that particular part of the kitchen, Brandon didn't want to wait around for another attack. He got Willa to her feet and opened the mudroom door so he could get her into the garage.

"What now?" she asked. She was still shivering, and Brandon prayed this stress and all the running around weren't harming the baby.

He glanced at the car and knew he had left the keys in the ignition. He could try to drive them out of there, but since the shooter was out front, that would almost certainly put them right back in the line of fire.

Plus, there was the possibility of a second vehicle. An accomplice who might be blocking the road to prevent them from getting away.

"We're going out back," Brandon whispered.

He tipped his head to the rear door that led into the backyard. Beyond that was a small barn and then the thick woods that made a semicircle around his property. If worse came to worst, there were plenty of hiding places in those woods. However, it would put Willa out there in the freezing night. Thank God she had on her coat, but that probably wouldn't be enough eventually.

No. He had to end this soon.

With his gun still drawn, Brandon unlocked and eased open the door. He peeked out but didn't see any signs of the shooter. He didn't want to wait to give the person time to get around the house, either. Or time to get to Willa and him. It was a good twenty feet to the barn, and the woods were another twenty feet or more beyond that.

"Let's go," he told Willa.

Brandon kept watch all around them. Or at least that's what he tried to do. Hard to cover all the shadows and places a killer could hide and launch a new attack. So, he focused on hurrying to get them to the side of the barn. They reached it.

Just as a bullet came their way.

Hell. The shooter had moved to the backyard and had a visual on them.

Brandon pulled Willa to the ground. The dirt was rock-hard frozen, so he tried to break her fall with his arm.

It wasn't a second too soon because the bullets slammed into the side of the barn. Not one shot but four before the gunman stopped.

Was he moving to a new position?

Brandon glanced out but couldn't see anyone. Worse, the wind was even louder outside so he wasn't even sure he could hear approaching footsteps. All he could do was wait and pray for a safe opening to get Willa into the woods.

"There," Willa whispered. Her voice was frantic enough that Brandon glanced at her to see where her attention and index finger were aimed.

She was pointing at the kitchen door, specifically at the small sidelight window.

He saw the movement. Inside the house.

Brandon shook his head. How the hell had the person gotten inside so quickly? Just seconds earlier, the shots had come from the right exterior side of the house.

Maybe this was an accomplice?

There was no way the county sheriff could have already made it out here.

Brandon's gaze fired all around, in case this was some kind of ploy to distract him. He damn sure didn't want the shooter sneaking up on them.

There was more movement from the sidelight window, and from the corner of his eye, Brandon saw the back door ease open.

With his heart in his throat, he levered himself up a little and took aim.

He didn't fire, just in case this was indeed the county sheriff. Instead, he waited.

Behind him Willa waited, too, and he thought he heard her mumble a prayer. Good. Because they might need divine intervention to get through this.

The door opened all the way, and Brandon saw the hand then. Whoever was in his kitchen was holding a gun.

Brandon watched as the figure stepped onto the porch.

It was a man, and like Brandon, he had his gun ready to fire.

"Brandon?" the man called out.

Hell.

And Willa obviously recognized him, too, because she cursed.

Sergeant Cash Newsome was on the porch.

That barely had time to register in Brandon's mind when the next shot rang out.

WILLA CAUGHT JUST A glimpse of Cash a split second before Brandon dropped back down in front of her. But a glimpse was all she needed to know that Cash was close enough to them to deliver a fatal shot.

If that was his intention.

Brandon fired in the direction of the shooter—still on the right rear of the house. The blast echoed in her ears. Because of her own pounding heartbeat, she was already having trouble hearing, and that certainly didn't help. However, Willa didn't need to hear to know that Brandon and she had to get out of there fast. With the shooter—and now perhaps Cash—they were outgunned. Sure, she had a gun, but she didn't trust her shooting skills against a cop.

"Brandon, Willa, I'm here to help you!" Cash called out.

Thank God Brandon didn't buy that because he began to scoot her toward the back side of the barn.

Away from Cash.

Hopefully, away from the other shooter, too.

There was another shot, but because Brandon was in the way, she couldn't see where this one landed. However, she heard Cash curse. He said something, too, something drowned out by the next shot.

Was this some kind of ploy by Cash to make them think he was innocent, or was he under fire just like them?

Brandon didn't wait to find out.

He got them to the back of the barn, keeping them

right at the corner, probably so they could duck around the side if the shooter came at them from either direction. The problem with that was ducking to the side could put them in Cash's sight again.

"We're going to the woods," Brandon whispered. "Stay behind me."

The woods. Well, at least there were plenty of huge trees that could hopefully absorb the bullets—she had no doubts that shooter would continue to fire at them.

Maybe Cash, too.

She got behind Brandon as he asked, and they started to walk backward toward the woods. Willa kept her gun ready and prayed she could do some good with it if it came down to the shooter or them.

The wind howled and slapped at them, and it robbed her of what little breath she had left. Still, she tried to keep walking, hurrying, while she kept watch all around them. Brandon kept watch, too, and he kept volleying his gun between the porch where Cash was and the general area where the shooter had fired the last shot.

Willa felt something soft but solid bump against the lower back part of her leg, and she nearly let out a yelp. She also tried not to trip, especially when Brandon walked right into her.

She risked glancing at what was on the ground and spotted one of the dogs.

Oh, God.

At first, she thought he was dead, but then she saw his chest pumping. The Doberman was taking in quick, shallow breaths.

"Someone drugged him," Brandon mumbled. He

turned, caught Willa's arm and practically ran with her to the nearest tree.

They ducked behind it.

"Will your dog be all right?" she asked.

"Maybe." But he didn't sound very hopeful.

Neither was she. Anyone who would try to murder a pregnant woman probably didn't have much value for life in general.

"We'll help him later," Brandon said.

Willa latched on to that thought. There would be a later. They would get out of this safely.

Brandon peered out from behind the tree but immediately popped back into cover. Someone fired a shot, slamming right into the tree where his head had been just seconds earlier. She didn't think it was her imagination that the shooter had moved closer.

"Watch out, Brandon!" Cash shouted.

That sent Willa's heart pumping even more, and she turned, looking all around them, but she didn't see anyone.

There was another shot, but it didn't hit the tree. In fact, she didn't think it had even been fired in their direction.

A moment later, she heard Cash moan.

The man sounded as if he were in pain. And maybe he was. Maybe he had been shot. Of course, it could all be an act to draw them out into the open so he could kill them.

All around them were the sounds of the wind assaulting the trees, and she couldn't pick through that noise and determine what the heck was going on, but she had a horrible gut feeling that things were about to get worse than they already were.

"Should we stay put?" she whispered.

Her voice was beyond shaky, and that must have been the reason he glanced back at her. "For now." Unlike her, his voice was calm.

Reassuring.

She thought of their short time together. It came like images flying through her mind. She'd only known Brandon for two days. That was it. Under normal circumstances, she would have considered him practically a stranger. But he wasn't. He was the father of her child and the only person she completely trusted.

And she was in love with him.

It was the worst possible time for that to pop into her head. She couldn't tell him, of course. That wasn't such a bad thing. Willa wasn't sure *I love you* was something Brandon would ever want to hear from her.

Maybe it was that particular heartbreaking thought that distracted her. Or maybe she truly didn't hear the sound of the footsteps.

But there had been footsteps. Unheard ones.

Willa had no doubt about that when she felt someone knock the weapon from her hand. She also felt herself being jerked backward.

Into someone's arms.

And before she could even call out, that someone put a gun to her head.

Chapter Seventeen

Brandon sensed the movement behind him and whirled in that direction.

But it was too late.

Someone had Willa.

His breath vanished. His stomach knotted. Hell, his heart nearly stopped. Because this was his worst-case scenario come true. The SOB who had been trying to kill them, now had control of the situation.

Brandon couldn't see the person's face, only the sleeve of a thick coat and the gloved hand that held a gun pressed up against Willa's right temple. The person's body and face were hidden behind the tree.

He made a split-second glance at the porch, the last place he'd seen Cash.

The man was no longer there.

Brandon cursed again. He hadn't seen Cash get up and leave, but then he hadn't exactly had all his attention focused on the porch, either. He'd known there might be two possible attackers, and he hadn't wanted to watch only Cash and give the second person a chance to sneak up on them.

But that's what had happened.

Or else maybe it was Cash who now had Willa.

Brandon didn't care who it was. He only wanted to get Willa away from that gun.

"Who are you, and what do you want?" Brandon asked the gunman.

The person didn't answer. Didn't move. Neither did Willa. Her entire body seemed frozen in place, and the only movement was from the wind whipping at her hair. Her eyes were wide, her mouth slightly open. She was obviously terrified, and while Brandon wanted to assure her that everything was going to be okay, he knew she wouldn't believe him. He didn't believe it, either.

There were no guarantees that either of them would make it out of this alive.

"Let Willa go," he tried again.

And he would keep on trying because there was no alternative. Somehow, he had to talk the person into dropping that gun, or else he had to use force to take it away. The longer this went on, the higher the chances that Willa would be hurt.

Or worse.

"Willa doesn't remember everything that happened in the hospital lab," Brandon continued. "She has no idea who hired the men who held her hostage."

There was only about eight feet of space between them, but Brandon inched closer. He had to get within reach of the gun, and lunging for it wouldn't work.

"Think of Willa's baby. My *baby*," he added. Saying those words cut deep into his heart because for the first time, he saw the baby. Not Willa's pregnant stomach. Not the vague images he'd tried to keep pushing away.

Brandon saw what it would be like to hold his child.

His daughter.

And if this gunman took Willa's life, then his baby wouldn't have a chance. Brandon wouldn't have the opportunity to tell Willa just how much she and this baby meant to him.

"Don't do this," Brandon pleaded. "Please, just let Willa go."

At first he thought his words were useless, that they were having no effect on the person. But then, he saw the slight movement of the trigger finger. The gunman's index finger tensed as if there were some hesitation. Maybe because the gunman hadn't considered just how difficult it was to threaten a woman and her unborn child.

"Let Willa go," Brandon repeated. "And if you need a hostage, take me. Better yet, just leave. Just get back in your car and put an end to this now."

Of course, Brandon couldn't let the person just drive away as if none of this had happened. He would have to stop this once and for all, otherwise the danger would continue. But for now he would say or do whatever it took to get Willa out of the line of fire.

Because Willa was staring at him, he had no trouble seeing when she lifted her left eyebrow. She seemed to be questioning him about what she should do. Maybe she was thinking about trying to drop to the ground so that Brandon could get a clean shot.

But he only shook his head.

If the gunman fired, there wouldn't be time for Willa

to move out of the way. It was too big of a risk to take, especially since he seemed to be making progress.

"I can help you," Brandon told the gunman. "I have money inside so you can get away. You can leave now, and no one else will get hurt."

If it was Cash behind that gun, he probably knew that wouldn't happen. But the other three—Wes, Dean and Dr. Farris—they might believe it.

And even Cash might *want* to believe it if he was trying to rationalize a way out of this.

Martin Shore had been a cold-blooded killer, an assassin, but none of the four suspects had likely done a close-kill attempt like this before. Brandon had. During his time in the military, he'd been forced into violent situations. And he knew it wasn't something that most people could stomach.

"Here's what we can do," Brandon continued. It was almost impossible to keep his voice level and calm, especially while looking in Willa's eyes, so he focused on the gunman's trigger finger. "We both put our guns down. We just drop them. Willa and I will get on the ground while you walk away."

The seconds crawled by.

The gunman still didn't utter a sound, but the gloved trigger finger lifted just a fraction. That certainly didn't mean Willa was out of danger, not by a long shot, but he was making progress.

"I want to name our daughter Hannah," Brandon said. It wasn't exactly the first name that came to mind, but it was a name he liked. "She'll be born in February."

The movement on Willa's face caused him to glance at her. She was blinking back tears.

But the gunman didn't have a tearful reaction. The finger went right back on the trigger, and Brandon thought the person was shaking his or her head.

Damn.

He had to say the right thing or do something, and it had to happen now. But what? How could he get through to this would-be killer?

Brandon didn't have a chance to figure that out.

He heard the sound and then saw the movement cut through the darkness. Something came flying through the air.

A small tree branch.

And it smacked right into the back of the gunman's head.

Everything happened fast. Too fast for Brandon to do anything but rely on his instincts to react.

The gunman made a feral sound, part gasp, part outrage. But somehow, the person managed to hang on to the gun.

That didn't stop Brandon.

He latched onto Willa's arm and slung her out of the way. It worked.

Well, it got Willa out of the way.

However, it didn't stop the other things that had already been set in motion.

Their assailant turned. And fired. Not at Willa or Brandon. But at the person who had just delivered that blow with the tree limb.

But before Brandon could take aim and right his own position, it was already too late. He found himself staring right down the barrel of their attacker's Sig-Sauer.

"Move and you die," the person warned.

THE SOUND OF THE VOICE caused Willa's breath to stall in her lungs. She instantly recognized the person who'd just issued Brandon that death threat.

When all of this had first started, she had thought it was Cash or Wes who was holding her at gunpoint. But it wasn't either of the men.

It was Dr. Lenora Farris.

Willa stared up from the ground where Brandon had pushed her out of the way, and she looked around. The gun that Dr. Farris had knocked from her hand minutes earlier was there, on the ground. Willa reached out for it.

"Don't," the doctor warned. It was hardly the caring, empathetic tone she'd used in the hotel suite when she had shown Willa that DVD.

The doctor grabbed Willa again and put her in front of her. She curved her arm around Willa's throat. The position literally made her a human shield. It would make it nearly impossible again for Brandon to fire.

While keeping the gun aimed at Willa's head, the doctor kicked away the gun that Willa had tried to reach. She also used her foot to swat at something else. Something near the tree limb that had hit Dr. Farris in the head.

"Why?" Willa asked, trying to look back at her so she could make eye contact. "You're the one who tried to help me regain my memory."

She gave a weary, hollow laugh and shifted her

position so that her back was against the tree. "I didn't want to help you. I was there to find out how much you knew. How much you remembered." The doctor glanced at her. "You remembered too much, Willa."

"Obviously not. Because I don't have a clue why you're doing this."

"Dr. Farris is doing it because she's trying to cover up her guilt," someone snarled.

It was Cash, and he was on the ground to the doctor's left. He sounded as if he was in pain, but it was too dark for Willa to see if he'd been hurt. Though he probably had been. After all, Cash was the one who had tried to hit the doctor with the tree limb, and she had fired in that direction. It was also likely his gun the doctor had kicked out of reach.

But Brandon was still armed. And maybe that's why the doctor turned the gun back on Willa. "Sheriff Ruiz, do as I say, if you want her to live."

Dr. Farris shot a glance Cash's way and what she saw must not have alarmed her enough to finish him off. Instead, she kept her attention nailed to Brandon.

"She put a tracking device on your car," Cash continued. Yes, he was definitely hurt, and he paused to pull in his breath between each word.

God, was he dying? Willa prayed not.

"Why don't you want Willa to remember?" Brandon asked. He stepped closer.

The doctor shook her head and thrust her gun at Willa's stomach. "Stay put and drop your gun," she warned Brandon. "I'm calling the shots here."

"Yeah," Cash agreed. "She's calling the shots because she's a killer. I didn't trust her when I saw that photo Dean had given you. She set me up with that picture. She called, said she had evidence about the case, but I'm guessing she did that so she could get something incriminating in case she needed a fall guy."

If so, then all of this had obviously been premeditated.

"That's why I followed her when she started driving out here toward your place," Cash added. "I figured she'd try to kill you."

Too bad Cash hadn't been able to stop her.

"Put. Down. Your. Gun." Dr. Farris's teeth were clenched when she threatened Brandon.

Willa didn't want him to drop the gun so she tried to help. It was obvious the doctor was far from being calm and in control. Her hands were shaking, and she looked to be on the verge of killing them all.

"The gunman in the lab wanted me to tamper with some DNA files," Willa said. It worked. The doctor went still. "It was the DNA taken from beneath Jessie Beecham's fingernails the night he was murdered."

That last part was a guess. But it was obviously a good one because Dr. Farris groaned softly. "You do remember," she mumbled. Now, there was sadness, maybe even regret, in her voice. "The DNA would have sent me to jail for murder. Because it was my skin tissue beneath Jessie's nails. He scratched me, and I didn't have time to clean him up."

"You killed Jessie Beecham," Willa mumbled. The next question was why, but Willa didn't get a chance to ask her that.

A weary sigh left the doctor's mouth, and she loosened the grip she had around Willa's neck. Since she wasn't watching Cash, Willa hoped the man wasn't so injured that he was unable to do something to help.

Without warning, the doctor pulled the trigger.

The sound blasted through the night, and Willa braced herself to die.

But the bullet slammed into the ground next to her. In the same motion, she swung the gun back to Brandon. "Put down your weapon, or I'll kill you both right now."

Brandon stared at the woman. And then he shook his head and cursed.

He dropped the gun.

Willa's heart dropped with it.

That gun was the only thing protecting them, but Brandon had had no choice. Willa didn't know the doctor very well, but she could tell from the woman's tone that she wasn't bluffing. Of course, Dr. Farris intended to kill them anyway so this would only give them a few more seconds at best.

"I won't go to jail for killing Jessie," the doctor said in an almost whisper. "The man was scum and deserved to die."

Maybe. But now, the doctor was apparently willing to keep on killing.

"I'm sorry," Dr. Farris added.

Everything happened fast. Practically a blur. Dr. Farris lifted her hand, aimed her gun back at Cash. She fired. Two shots. Both slammed into something.

Cash, probably.

The doctor didn't waste even a second. She took aim at Brandon. She was going to fire. Willa had no doubt about that. The doctor was going to shoot Brandon at point-blank range, and he was helpless, standing there, because he couldn't risk coming at the doctor and hurting Willa.

But Willa could do something.

Yes, it was a risk. Anything was at this point. But she couldn't just stand there and let Brandon die.

Willa gathered the air into her lungs and let out the loudest yell she could manage. She threw all of her weight to the left, away from the doctor. The jarring motion worked because Dr. Farris's arm snapped back, releasing the grip she had on Willa's neck. At first, Willa wasn't sure why that had happened.

Then, she saw Brandon.

He had lunged across the space that separated him from the doctor. He was obviously trying to tackle her before she got off another shot.

But he was too late.

The blast, loud and thick, tore through the night.

Everything seemed to freeze, and the images clicked through her head as if someone was snapping pictures. Willa saw Brandon slam into Dr. Farris, and they both flew backward, tumbling onto the ground.

Then, Willa saw the blood.

It was everywhere. On Brandon. On Dr. Farris. Even in the evening light, she could see it on both their clothes.

"Brandon!" Willa called out. He had to be all right. He just had to be. She couldn't lose him.

She scrambled across the yard toward the scuffle. Brandon had the doctor in a fierce grip, his left hand locked around her arm, and his right hand gripped her weapon. And she was fighting back. Though not with much strength.

Willa soon saw why.

Behind Brandon and Dr. Farris, Cash was sitting up, and there was blood all over the front of his shirt. No doubt where Dr. Farris had shot him. He had a gun. The gun that the doctor had knocked from Willa's hand. And judging from the angle of the barrel, he had fired directly at Dr. Farris.

But Brandon had also been in that line of fire.

For one terrifying moment, Willa thought Cash might fire again. At her or at Brandon. But he simply gave a satisfied nod before he collapsed, the gun falling to his side.

Cash might be dead. That registered in Willa's mind. But she couldn't go to him until she helped Brandon. She couldn't let Dr. Farris use that gun to kill him.

Willa reached out to latch on to the doctor's arm so she could help drag the woman away from Brandon. But the arm she held was limp and lifeless.

Willa's gaze flew to Brandon. To his face. To his body. Yes, there was blood. But when he stood, she realized he hadn't been shot. Dr. Farris had been. Cash's bullet had taken out a killer.

And Brandon was safe.

He was safe.

The tears came, burning hot in her eyes, and Willa made it to him in one step. Brandon pulled her warm and deep into his arms and held on.

Chapter Eighteen

Brandon glanced at his watch. It was still five minutes until midnight. Five minutes until it was officially Christmas Day.

Not that they would go anywhere to celebrate.

He didn't intend to leave the hospital until Cash was out of surgery. After all, Cash had probably saved their lives, and Brandon wanted to thank his old friend. However, that didn't mean Willa had to be stuck in an uncomfortable chair in the waiting room.

"Sheila said she could drive you to her place here in town so you can get some sleep," Brandon reminded Willa. It'd been a generous offer from his deputy, but both Sheila and Pete were probably reeling from everything that had happened.

Brandon certainly was.

Judging from Willa's too-pale face and trembling hands, she was as well.

"No thanks," she answered. "I'd rather wait here with you until the doctor gives us an update on Cash."

Since Cash had already been in surgery for hours, Brandon had no idea how much longer their wait would be. So he slipped his arm around her and eased her head onto his shoulder. Maybe she would at least grab a nap.

Or not.

Her head came right back up, and her eyes met his. "Dr. Farris deserved what she got."

"Yeah." Brandon didn't dispute that. The woman had tried to commit premeditated murder, and from what he'd been able to figure out from the notes and emails that SAPD had found on the doctor's computer, she'd taken plenty of steps to do just that.

Thank God she hadn't succeeded.

But not for lack of trying.

In addition to hiring Martin Shore to find and kill Willa, she had spied on Cash's computer to find the location of the safe house where Willa and he had been attacked. Cash had been right about that. He'd also been right about the doctor planting a tracking device on Brandon's vehicle. And to insure that Brandon's deputies wouldn't respond to his call for backup, the doctor had planted a jammer at the sheriff's office where the deputies were wrapping up Shore's last attack and death. The jammer had prevented their cell phones from ringing. She had even drugged his dogs so they wouldn't alert anyone that she was on his property.

Dr. Farris had been thorough. And in doing so, she had created plenty of future nightmares. Brandon would never forget how close he had come to losing Willa and the baby.

Brandon heard the footsteps in the corridor and got to his feet. He also tried to brace himself for the worst. Cash had not only taken three bullets, he'd lost a lot of blood.

But it wasn't the doctor. It was Pete.

"Merry Christmas," the deputy greeted, though it wasn't very cheery. The fatigue was heavy in Pete's weathered eyes.

"Merry Christmas," Brandon and Willa mumbled back.

"SAPD just called," Pete explained. "They tried your cell first, but the call couldn't go through in here."

Brandon was aware of that. Because the waiting room was right next to radiology, the walls had been reinforced with steel, making reception poor at best. Still, he figured his deputies would keep him informed, and they had. During Cash's three hours of surgery, either Pete or Sheila had paid them a visit at least every half hour.

"SAPD found more stuff on Dr. Farris's computer," Pete continued. He shook his head. "That woman was something else. One of the gunmen who took the maternity hostages was her patient, so she learned about the hostage situation before it even happened. But she didn't lift a finger to stop it."

That sent a coil of anger through Brandon. Willa had gone through hell and nearly died while as a hostage, and it could have been stopped before it even started.

Of course, if it had, he might never have met Willa and known about the baby.

Ironic that Willa was here in his arms because of Dr. Farris and those hostage-taking gunmen.

"So, if she knew the gunmen, was she also the one who hired them?" Willa asked.

"I guess you could say she just paid them to do something extra. Their boss had already hired them to tamper with some evidence, and Dr. Farris just paid them on the side to do the same for her. She had her DNA replaced with tissue from the homeless man who was arrested for Jessie Beecham's murder."

"A murder that Dr. Farris committed," Willa mumbled. "Yes. That woman was indeed something else."

Brandon agreed. But this might not be over. "What about the other hostage situation, the one that's supposed to happen today?"

"It was a lie," Pete insisted. "Well, according to the notes SAPD found, it was. She hired Shore to kill Willa and to also get out the word that there'd be another set of hostages taken. But the story was just a ruse to draw Willa out of hiding."

Brandon cursed. The ruse had worked.

"There won't be any other hostages," Willa said. And she repeated it. The breath just swooshed out of her, and when she looked at Brandon, he saw her smile. It was, well, amazing and it lit up her entire face.

Suddenly, it felt like Christmas morning.

"Y'all need me to bring you anything?" Pete asked.

Willa shook her head, but she didn't take her eyes off Brandon. "It's really over. No more danger. No more hostages. I'm free."

"The danger and hostage parts are true. But what about your memory?" Pete asked.

She paused a moment, as if going through her thoughts. "Everything seems to be there. I'm free," Willa repeated. "For the first time in months, I'm really free."

Yeah. And that hit him like a sucker punch.

Brandon was sure he wasn't smiling, and that warm Christmas glow faded as quickly as it'd come.

Willa was indeed free, and that meant she could and probably would be leaving soon. Of course, that left Brandon with a huge question.

Was he going to let her go?

It took him about a split second to come up the answer to that.

No. He wasn't going to let her go.

Well, not without a fight anyway.

"I know I said I might not make a good father," Brandon heard himself blurt out. Not the best start he could have had for what would be the most important next few minutes of his life.

"But I'd like to try," Brandon added.

Willa blinked. Stared at him.

"Uh, I should probably go," Pete mumbled. And he didn't wait for either of them to acknowledge his exit. Being the smart man that he was, Pete left Brandon to fumble around with what he wanted to say to Willa.

"I'd like to try to be a good father," Brandon amended. He shook his head. That still wasn't right. "I'll do everything within my power to be a good father."

"To Hannah," she supplied, making it sound like more of a question than clarification.

"Hannah." He huffed. And then cursed when Willa looked hurt from that huff. "No. I didn't mean it that way. I used the name, Hannah, to make the baby more personal to Dr. Farris, so she wouldn't shoot you. It's a hostage negotiation technique to personalize the crisis situation."

Great. Now, he was babbling.

"But I do like the name Hannah," he added when Willa just stared at him.

Still babbling.

So, Brandon changed tactics. He cradled the back of Willa's neck and pulled her closer. He kissed her. Really kissed her. He put his mouth to hers and took in the softness of her lips. Her taste. That taste soothed him, fired his blood and reminded him just what was at stake here.

Everything was at stake.

"I'm in love with you," he said against her mouth.

He braced himself for her shock and expected her to pull back and stare at him some more. After all, he'd given her no indication of that love. Hell, he hadn't realized himself until he saw Dr. Farris point the gun at her. Then, in that moment, he knew this wasn't about protecting Willa and the baby.

It was about loving them.

Willa didn't pull back, but he felt her smile form on her lips. "You love me?"

Well, this answer was easy. "I do."

"Good." And she kissed him long and hard and stopped only when both of them remembered they needed to breathe. "Because I'm love in with you, too."

The breath he'd just taken in stalled in his throat. His entire body seemed to stop, so he could grasp what she'd just said.

"You love me?" he clarified.

"God, yes. I thought that was way too obvious."

Now, it was his turn to smile against her mouth. But

Brandon did ease back because he wanted to see her face. Her eyes. That incredible smile. Willa took his breath away again, and he didn't care if he ever got it back.

Maybe it was because he was totally lost in the moment that he didn't hear the footsteps until they stopped right next to him.

Brandon caught the movement out of the corner of his eye and automatically reached for his weapon. But no weapon was necessary. It was Dr. Ross Jenkins, the surgeon who had been operating on Cash.

Both Brandon and Willa got to their feet, and Brandon tried to interpret the surgeon's poker face. He couldn't. He could only stand there and wait.

"Sergeant Newsome took three bullets to the chest cavity. He's lucky. Damn lucky. Other than a collapsed lung and some broken ribs, he should be fine."

The relief was instant, and Brandon grabbed Willa and hauled her into his arms for a celebratory kiss. Cash was going to be all right. Dr. Farris hadn't succeeded in any part of her plan to kill all three of them.

"I'll keep him sedated most of the day," the doctor continued. "No visitors until tomorrow. So, you two might as well go home." His attention dropped to Willa's belly. "Do I need to call in the OB?"

"No," Willa quickly answered. "No contractions. And Hannah's kicking like crazy. She's fine."

The doctor nodded, pulled on his surgical cap and ambled away.

Willa smiled again, but there were tears in her eyes. "Cash is going to be okay," she mumbled.

Brandon understood those tears. They were of the

happy variety. And even though the timing wasn't the best, he decided to see if there was another level of happy to be had here.

But before he could utter a word, Willa pulled back her shoulders and stared at him. "Are you going to ask me to marry you?"

He had been about to do just that, but Brandon hadn't expected her to jump the gun. And he couldn't tell if it was a question she wanted him to ask. The tears were still there in her eyes, but she was no longer smiling.

She was waiting.

It was a risk because if she said no, she might feel too awkward to hang around. She might say they needed space, time or some other thing that Brandon was sure he didn't want.

He wanted Willa.

He wanted their daughter.

And he had never been so sure of anything in his entire life.

To increase her chances of saying yes, he snapped her back to him for a kiss. He made it long, French and hopefully as mind-numbing as he could manage. Willa added some mind numbing moves of her own and pressed herself against him. Hard against him. In such a way that reminded him that he could spend at least part of Christmas day making love to her.

But first, he needed to ask the question.

And get the answer.

He caught on her shoulders and looked her straight in the eyes. "Willa, will you—"

"Yes," she interrupted. She grabbed a handful of his shirt and dragged him right back to her.

But Brandon wasn't sure exactly what question she was answering. "Yes?" he quizzed. He stepped back a little so he could keep a clear head.

Her smile returned. So did the kiss. "Yes, I'll marry you, Brandon. I'll be your wife. Your lover. The mother of your children. Yes to all of it."

That was the only answer he wanted.

So, Brandon pulled her to him and kissed the start of their new life together.

* * * * *

*Next month, look for WILD STALLION,
the next book in Delores Fossen's miniseries*
TEXAS MATERNITY: LABOR AND DELIVERY,
wherever Harlequin Intrigue books are sold!

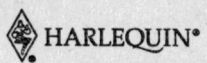
HARLEQUIN®

INTRIGUE®

COMING NEXT MONTH

Available December 7, 2010

#1245 MAN WITH THE MUSCLE
Bodyguard of the Month
Julie Miller

#1246 WINCHESTER CHRISTMAS WEDDING
Whitehorse, Montana: Winchester Ranch Reloaded
B.J. Daniels

#1247 COLBY CORE
Colby Agency: Christmas Miracles
Debra Webb

#1248 WILD STALLION
Texas Maternity: Labor and Delivery
Delores Fossen

#1249 GENUINE COWBOY
Sons of Troy Ledger
Joanna Wayne

#1250 A SILVERHILL CHRISTMAS
Carol Ericson

REQUEST YOUR FREE BOOKS!

2 FREE NOVELS PLUS 2 FREE GIFTS!

 HARLEQUIN®
INTRIGUE®

Breathtaking Romantic Suspense

YES! Please send me 2 FREE Harlequin Intrigue® novels and my 2 FREE gifts (gifts are worth about $10). After receiving them, if I don't wish to receive any more books, I can return the shipping statement marked "cancel." If I don't cancel, I will receive 6 brand-new novels every month and be billed just $4.24 per book in the U.S. or $4.99 per book in Canada. That's a saving of at least 15% off the cover price! It's quite a bargain! Shipping and handling is just 50¢ per book.* I understand that accepting the 2 free books and gifts places me under no obligation to buy anything. I can always return a shipment and cancel at any time. Even if I never buy another book from Harlequin, the two free books and gifts are mine to keep forever.

182/382 HDN E5MG

Name _____ (PLEASE PRINT) _____

Address _____ Apt. #

City _____ State/Prov. _____ Zip/Postal Code

Signature (if under 18, a parent or guardian must sign)

Mail to the **Harlequin Reader Service:**
IN U.S.A.: P.O. Box 1867, Buffalo, NY 14240-1867
IN CANADA: P.O. Box 609, Fort Erie, Ontario L2A 5X3

Not valid for current subscribers to Harlequin Intrigue books.

Are you a subscriber to Harlequin Intrigue books and want to receive the larger-print edition? Call 1-800-873-8635 today!

* Terms and prices subject to change without notice. Prices do not include applicable taxes. N.Y. residents add applicable sales tax. Canadian residents will be charged applicable provincial taxes and GST. Offer not valid in Quebec. This offer is limited to one order per household. All orders subject to approval. Credit or debit balances in a customer's account(s) may be offset by any other outstanding balance owed by or to the customer. Please allow 4 to 6 weeks for delivery. Offer available while quantities last.

Your Privacy: Harlequin is committed to protecting your privacy. Our Privacy Policy is available online at www.eHarlequin.com or upon request from the Reader Service. From time to time we make our lists of customers available to reputable third parties who may have a product or service of interest to you. If you would prefer we not share your name and address, please check here. ☐

Help us get it right—We strive for accurate, respectful and relevant communications. To clarify or modify your communication preferences, visit us at www.ReaderService.com/consumerschoice.

HI10R

A Romance

FOR EVERY MOOD™

Spotlight on
Classic

Quintessential, modern love stories
that are romance at its finest.

See the next page
to enjoy a sneak peek from
the Harlequin® Romance series.

*See below for a sneak peek from our classic
Harlequin® Romance® line.*

Introducing DADDY BY CHRISTMAS by Patricia Thayer.

MIA caught sight of Jarrett when he walked into the open lobby. It was hard not to notice the man. In a charcoal business suit with a crisp white shirt and striped tie covered by a dark trench coat, he looked more Wall Street than small-town Colorado.

Mia couldn't blame him for keeping his distance. He was probably tired of taking care of her.

Besides, why would a man like Jarrett McKane be interested in her? Why would he want to take on a woman expecting a baby? Yet he'd done so many things for her. He'd been there when she'd needed him most. How could she not care about a man like that?

Heart pounding in her ears, she walked up behind him. Jarrett turned to face her. "Did you get enough sleep last night?"

"Yes, thanks to you," she said, wondering if he'd thought about their kiss. Her gaze went to his mouth, then she quickly glanced away. "And thank you for not bringing up my meltdown."

Jarrett couldn't stop looking at Mia. Blue was definitely her color, bringing out the richness of her eyes.

"What meltdown?" he said, trying hard to focus on what she was saying. "You were just exhausted from lack of sleep and worried about your baby."

He couldn't help remembering how, during the night, he'd kept going in to watch her sleep. How strange was that? "I hope you got enough rest."

She nodded. "Plenty. And you're a good neighbor for

coming to my rescue."

He tensed. Neighbor? *What neighbor kisses you like I did?* "That's me, just the full-service landlord," he said, trying to keep the sarcasm out of his voice. He started to leave, but she put her hand on his arm.

"Jarrett, what I meant was you went beyond helping me." Her eyes searched his face. "I've asked far too much of you."

"Did you hear me complain?"

She shook her head. "You should. I feel like I've taken advantage."

"Like I said, I haven't minded."

"And I'm grateful for everything…"

Grasping her hand on his arm, Jarrett leaned forward. The memory of last night's kiss had him aching for another. "I didn't do it for your gratitude, Mia."

Gorgeous tycoon Jarrett McKane has never believed in Christmas—but he can't help being drawn to soon-to-be-mom Mia Saunders! Christmases past were spent alone…and now Jarrett may just have a fairy-tale ending for all his Christmases future!

Available December 2010, only from Harlequin® Romance®.

Silhouette *Desire*

USA TODAY bestselling authors

MAUREEN CHILD

and

SANDRA HYATT

UNDER THE MILLIONAIRE'S MISTLETOE

Just when these leading men thought they had it all figured out, they quickly learn their hearts have made other plans. Two passionate stories about love, longing and the infinite possibilities of kissing under the mistletoe.

Available December
wherever you buy books.

Always Powerful, Passionate and Provocative.

Visit Silhouette Books at www.eHarlequin.com